Dear Reader,

I just wanted to tell you how delighted I am that my publisher has decided to reprint so many of my earlier books. Some of them have not been available for a while, and amongst them there are titles that have often been requested.

I can't remember a time when I haven't written, although it was not until my daughter was born that I felt confident enough to attempt to get anything published. With my husband's encouragement, my first book was accepted, and since then there have been over 130 more.

Not that the thrill of having a book published gets any less. I still feel the same excitement when a new manuscript is accepted. But it's you, my readers, to whom I owe so much. Your support—and particularly your letters—give me so much pleasure.

I hope you enjoy this collection of some of my favourite novels.

Anne Mather

Back by Popular Demand

With a phenomenal one hundred and thirty books published by Mills & Boon, Anne Mather is one of the world's most popular romance authors. Mills & Boon are proud to bring back many of these highly sought-after novels in a special collector's edition.

ANNE MATHER: COLLECTOR'S EDITION

1 JAKE HOWARD'S WIFE
2 SCORPIONS' DANCE
3 CHARADE IN WINTER
4 A FEVER IN THE BLOOD
5 WILD ENCHANTRESS
6 SPIRIT OF ATLANTIS
7 LOREN'S BABY
8 DEVIL IN VELVET
9 LIVING WITH ADAM
10 SANDSTORM
11 A HAUNTING COMPULSION
12 IMAGES OF LOVE
13 FALLEN ANGEL
14 TRIAL OF INNOCENCE
15 THE MEDICI LOVER
16 THE JUDAS TRAP
17 PALE ORCHID
18 CAROLINE
19 THE SHROUDED WEB
20 A TRIAL MARRIAGE

IMAGES OF LOVE

BY
ANNE MATHER

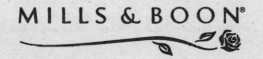

First published in Great Britain 1980 by Mills & Boon Limited
This edition 1998
Harlequin Mills & Boon Limited,
Eton House, 18-24 Paradise Road, Richmond, Surrey TW9 1SR

© Anne Mather 1980

ISBN 0 263 80563 8

Set in Times Roman 11 on 11½ pt by
Rowland Phototypesetting Limited
Bury St Edmunds, Suffolk

74-9802-49160

Made and printed in Great Britain by
Caledonian International Book Manufacturing Ltd, Glasgow

CHAPTER ONE

THROUGHOUT the journey, Mark had been abnormally quiet for him, and while the ocean beneath the powerful aircraft changed from silver-grey to turquoise blue, Tobie had plenty of time to re-examine her feelings. She wasn't just using Mark as an instrument of revenge, she told herself fiercely, she really cared about him, and her only reasons for agreeing to this trip were the usual ones of wanting to see his home and meet his mother. It was not an attempt to get even with anyone, and no matter what Laura might say, she was only trying to find the happiness that had so long been denied her. If——and here she allowed a tiny grain of self-justification to creep in——*if* she did feel a trace of mild self-satisfaction at the prospect of confronting Robert again, that was surely forgivable. After all, she had nothing to be ashamed of, and if she gave him a few uncomfortable moments, so much the better after the trauma she had gone through. It would be undeniably good to let him see that she had quite recovered from that wild infatuation, and she could even be grateful now that their relationship had not been legalised. A marriage, albeit a broken one, would have been that much harder to explain to Mark. As it was, he only knew there had once been someone else, but not that person's identity. It was a gamble, of course, taking the chance that Robert would not betray her, but as it would also mean betraying his brother, she felt reasonably confident.

Nevertheless, she could still hear her sister's shocked reaction when she first learned who Mark really was.

'So you're actually going to Emerald Cay to see Robert Lang again!' Laura had accused angrily. 'Oh, Tobie, how can you? Hasn't he humiliated you enough? What are you—one of those girls who enjoys punishment?'

'Of course not.' Tobie had denied the indictment indignantly. 'That would be foolish, wouldn't it? You know I care for Mark now. I'm going to Emerald Cay with him—to meet his mother. Whatever was between Robert and me is over.'

'But you do expect to see him, don't you?' Laura had persisted impatiently. 'How do you think he's going to react when he finds out who you are?'

'I imagine he knows,' Tobie retorted tautly, bending her head so that the silken weight of straight dark hair fell about her ears. 'After all, Mark and I are practically engaged! And my name's not so common. I should think Robert realised from the beginning, but do you honestly think he could come right out and say I'm the girl he virtually abandoned?'

Laura sighed, staring at her younger sister with troubled anxious eyes. 'Even so,' she said doubtfully, 'the man's unscrupulous, Tobie. We both know that. And this is his home you're invading. Emerald Cay belongs to him, doesn't it?'

'I believe so.' Tobie had shrugged, hoping to conclude the conversation. 'He went to live there—oh, about three years ago. Just after—just after the accident.'

Laura shook her head. 'Tobie! Change your mind. Don't go. This trip—it isn't good for you, I know it. You're recovered now, I know, but I just feel it in my bones—you're playing with fire! Tell Mark you can't go. Give yourself more time. Don't risk everything again. . .'

'It's no risk, Laura.' Tobie had spoken purposely lightly, but as the blue-green waters of the Caribbean unfolded beneath her, she wished she still felt so sure.

'We're almost there, darling.'

Mark's voice spoke near her ear, his breath fanning the tender lip of flesh, its warmth melting the chilling goosebumps that had unexpectedly appeared. It restored her sense of balance, reminding her that she was not alone any more, reassuring her of his love and affection. She had been uncertain about the trip in the beginning, but Mark's eagerness had persuaded her, and if she was going to marry him, sooner or later she would have to meet the other members of his family.

'You seem—anxious,' he said now, touching her chin, turning her face to his. 'You've no reason to be. My mother's going to love you. And Rob—' Tobie stiffened. 'Well, I guess we can talk about Rob tonight.'

His words had a slightly ominous ring, and Tobie's confidence faltered. 'Tonight?' she echoed, and Mark touched her nose with a playful finger.

'You know we're spending tonight in Castries,' he reminded her, mentioning the name of the island capital of St Lucia, the nearest large island to Emerald Cay, but Tobie was still apprehensive.

'Why—why should we have to talk about—about your half-brother?' she persisted, circling her dry lips with her tongue, and with a sigh Mark relaxed back in his seat.

'I've been trying to think of a way to explain him to you,' he confessed, unknowingly supplying the reason why Tobie had thought he had been unusually silent during the flight. 'Rob—well, Rob can be a law unto himself, and it isn't always enough just to put it down to his artistic temperament.'

Tobie's palms smoothed the arms of her seat. 'No?'

'No.'

She hesitated. 'You're—you're saying—he's conceited?'

'Hell, no!' Mark was swift to deny this. 'No one could call my brother conceited. But he can be rude—ignorant—bloody-minded, if you like. He—well, he doesn't always mince his words.' He sighed. 'He used not to be like that. I mean,' he hastened on quickly, 'he never suffered fools gladly, if you know what I mean, but since the accident—'

Tobie drew in an unsteady breath. 'I thought he got over that.'

'He did.' Mark sighed again. 'At least, as well as anyone could who was left in a wheelchair—'

'A *wheelchair*!' Tobie was all attention now, turning to stare at him with wide disbelieving eyes. 'Robert's *disabled*!'

'Don't use that word to him, honey, will you?' Mark advised her gently. 'It's not the sort of term you use where my brother is concerned. He's not an invalid, or so he says, he's only—somewhat incapacitated.'

Tobie could feel all the colour draining out of her face, and it was all she could do not to turn to Mark and beg him to take back his words. But she could say nothing. So far as Mark was concerned, she had not even met his brother, and although his revelation was both terrible and shocking, she must somehow sustain it without giving in to the shaking disbelief that gripped her. Yet she could hardly think straight as images of the man he had been flashed before her eyes. Robert—in a wheelchair! Robert—without the use of his legs! Robert, who had loved walking and driving, swimming and dancing. . .

'I know it's not generally known, that's why I wanted to warn you.' Fortunately Mark had warmed to his subject, and was paying her scant attention at the moment. 'That was Rob's idea, of course. If there's one thing he can't stand, it's sympathy, and you can imagine the worldwide reaction if it was discovered that Robert Lang had been crippled in a car crash. That was why he bought Emerald Cay, why he's dropped his public image. Not because he wanted to devote more time to his painting.'

Tobie felt totally drained of energy. Her whole body had slumped in her seat, and even her ankles felt weak. She couldn't believe it; she simply couldn't believe it. It explained so many things, and yet left so many others unexplained.

'Anyway, it's not so bad now,' Mark added thoughtfully. 'I mean, he still has the wheelchair around, but it's not his only means of getting about. He manages pretty well on sticks these days. Not that he advertises that fact either. It's a bit of a struggle, if you know what I mean, and like I said, Rob hates sympathy.'

Then, as if just realising that after her first horrified reaction Tobie had said nothing, he half turned towards her, grimacing when he saw her white face.

'Hey,' he exclaimed generously, 'there's no need for you to feel so badly, honey. I know you're a fan of his and all, but really, it hasn't affected his work, and that's the important thing, isn't it? You've seen his latest exhibition. His talent's still as great as it ever was.'

Tobie knew she had to say something, but the words were so hard to articulate. 'It—I—you should have told me sooner, Mark,' she got out at last. 'I—I don't know what to say.'

'Does it matter?' Mark made a sound of impatience. 'Come on! It's nothing to do with us, is it? I just didn't want you to—well, say something you might regret.'

'Regret?' Tobie echoed weakly, wishing suddenly that she had listened to Laura.

'Seeing him in a wheelchair for the first time,' Mark explained softly. 'I don't want you to be hurt. And Rob can be so damned sarcastic to people who show any sign of compassion!'

'Can he?'

Tobie felt totally incapable of handling the situation. She only knew that if she had known about this before leaving London, she would never have agreed to come. She didn't know why exactly. It didn't change anything, so far as she and Mark were concerned. But somehow her presence seemed ghoulish now, an unwanted and unwarranted reminder of the past; and while she admitted that her feelings for Robert had died on the operating table more than three years ago, she was loath to arouse emotions that could only cause him bitterness.

'You knew about the accident,' Mark probed now, and she managed to nod. It would have been foolish to state otherwise. It had been in all the papers, and as Mark had said, she was a fan. 'Anyway, it all happened a long time ago,' he reassured her, and she guessed his patience was wearing a little thin. 'There's no reason for you to get upset about it. It was his own fault. He was driving too fast as usual. That damned car of his—' He shook his head. 'Who needs a car that can do nearly two hundred miles an hour on roads where the speed limit is seventy?'

Tobie swallowed convulsively. 'Some—some people like fast cars,' she offered feebly, remembering the Porsche only too well. She remembered, too, the reason he had been driving fast, and that last terrible row before he left her. . .

'If you had to patch them up afterwards, perhaps you wouldn't speak so carelessly,' Mark remarked now, his tone full of indignation. 'We see them all at the hospital. Young men, girls, kids, most of them, with too much power under the bonnet and too little grey matter in their skulls. Losing a leg or an arm, or their sight. And they're the lucky ones. Paralysis is the most likely result, and believe me, it's not a pretty sight.'

Tobie shook her head. 'I—I didn't mean—'

'I know you didn't.' Mark's smile suddenly illuminated his fair handsome face. 'I guess Rob's accident happened around the time we first met, didn't it? And at that time you were in no fit state to be aware of anyone's troubles but your own.'

No fit state. . .

Hysteria swelled inside her. If he only knew, she thought sickly. If he ever found out. . .

'Not that I was involved with his recovery,' Mark continued. 'He wasn't a patient of mine.' He shrugged. 'There was one consolation, though. It did bring him and my mother together again. You don't know this, but before the accident they were a little less than close!'

Tobie bent her head. She wondered how Mark would react if she told him that she *had* known that. That in fact she had been staggered when she learned that after all that Robert had told her about his mother, he had actually forgiven her at last. He had always maintained that would never happen. But circumstances alter cases, she thought unsteadily, the weight of what she had learned bearing heavily on her.

'So. . .' Mark's smile appeared again, 'I've told you. I knew I'd have to, but—well, it's not easy, destroying an ideal.'

An ideal! Tobie turned to stare out of the window, and as she did so, the stewardess advised the passengers to fasten their safety belts and put out their cigarettes ready for landing at Hewanorra airport. Was that how Mark imagined she thought of his brother? How differently he would have felt if he had known the truth. And how differently might she have reacted if she had suspected that Robert had not made a complete recovery?

The hotel in Castries was air-conditioned and very comfortable, and Tobie had no objections when Mark suggested that they rested for a couple of hours before dinner. It had been a long flight, and a long drive, and although it was only early evening in the Caribbean, her body told her it was much later in London.

Mark had booked adjoining rooms, but as yet he had not tried to force their relationship. He wanted to make love to her, she knew that, but being a doctor, he was also aware of the reasons why she had refused to allow him to do so. Since Robert, since the emotional impact of what had happened to her, she found it incredibly difficult to relate to any man in a physical way, and Mark was sensible enough to see that if he compelled her to respond to him, he might destroy the tenuous thread he had constructed. So they remained friends, but not lovers in the true sense of the word, and Tobie believed they were closer than she and Robert had ever been.

Lying on her bed, however, with the blinds drawn against the lighted street outside, and the steady hum of the hotel drifting irresistibly to her ears, she found it impossible to relax. Everything Mark had told her went round and round in her head, until she felt almost dizzy with the perplexity of her thoughts. Robert was an invalid, or he was crippled, at least. All those nightmares she had had during her illness, the women she had used to torment herself he was spending his nights with, had only existed in her imagination. She could understand why Mark had felt it necessary to warn her about the uncertainty of his moods. Robert had always been an arrogant devil, and even now she found it almost impossible to picture him any other way.

She remembered the first time she had met him, when he came striding into the gallery where she worked. Her boss, Vincent Thomas, was staging one of his exhibitions, but she had not known that the tall lean stranger in the shabby denim shirt and jeans was Robert Lang. All she had seen was a man in his early thirties, a dark man, with untidy black hair, and skin with an olive cast. She had at first taken him for an intruder, not altogether trusting the way his dark eyes had swiftly appraised the layout of the gallery, and the general accessibility of the paintings, half suspecting he was checking the place out with criminal intent. Even when the dark eyes turned in her direction, and she found her own body betraying the dictates of her common sense, she was loath to admit that she found him disturbing, but when he spoke she was incapable of voicing any reproof. Robert had an attractive voice, low and mellow, with just a hint of the humour he had possessed in such measure, providing a lighter tone. And her nervousness had amused him, she had known that, even before he spoke to her and asked her who she was.

She had answered him. How could she not? She was in charge of the gallery in Vincent's absence, and for all she knew, this man might be a valued customer. But when it became apparent that he was more interested in her than the paintings, she had made a polite withdrawal, leaving him to browse around alone.

He was gone before Vincent returned, and although she knew she ought to mention the suspicious circumstances of his visit, she was curiously unwilling to do so. Instead she kept the encounter to herself, and worried herself sick that night in case there should be a break-in.

The following afternoon he was waiting for her when she left her office. She hardly recognised him in a well cut navy lounge suit, but when she did, she was astounded at his audacity. All her earlier doubts returned, and she convinced herself he intended to incriminate her in some plot to rob the gallery.

His suggestion that she joined him for a drink

before going home both excited and frightened
her. She wanted to go with him, she knew that,
but she also believed she was playing with fire,
though how much, she had yet to learn.

In the event, she had agreed to accompany him
to a club nearby, the exclusiveness of its clientele
only occurring to her when she was seated on a
plush stool at the bar. It was difficult to think of
anything with his dark eyes playing lazily over
her face, lingering longer than was necessary on
her mouth, before returning to tantalise the dart-
ing uncertainty of hers. She had never met anyone
quite like him before, and her lips twisted now
when she remembered how naïve she must have
seemed.

'Tell me about yourself,' he prompted, when
she had taken possession of a tall glass of
Campari soda—her choice, not his—and she had
found herself explaining that although she had
been born in Northumberland, since her parents'
death two years ago she had been living with her
married sister, Laura, in Wimbledon.

'And you've worked at the gallery how long?'
he probed, studying her expression, and she
admitted she had only been there a little over six
months, having spent her first year in London,
taking a secretarial course.

'I thought I hadn't seen you there before,' he
remarked, surprising her, and Tobie thought it
was time she asked some questions of her own.

'What—er—what do you do, Mr—Mr—' she
had begun awkwardly, realising she didn't even

know his name, and his dark brows had drawn together aggressively.

'You mean you don't know?' he asked, his expression coldly sceptical, and she had had her first glimpse of another side to his character.

'No,' she insisted, glancing uneasily about her. 'Why should I?'

Robert had looked at her sharply, as if gauging her sincerity, and then, without provocation, he demanded: 'So what the hell are you doing, accepting invitations from strange men? Didn't that sister of yours tell you anything?'

His attack was so unexpected, Tobie was stunned by it. One minute they had been sitting enjoying a quiet drink together, and the next his dark face was contorted with anger, his lips thin and impatient. More than anything, it convinced her of the veracity of his words, and she fumbled desperately for her handbag, jumping down from her stool, and charging out of the club as if the devil himself was at her heels.

And he was—or so she thought when Robert caught up with her in the narrow side street adjoining the main thoroughfare. His face was grim and unrepentant, and the fingers that closed over her wrist were as hard and relentless as any tool of torture might be.

'What the hell do you think you're doing?' he had exhorted, swinging her round to face him, and despite her tearful mortification, the desire to leave him melted beneath the powerful attraction he exerted.

'I—I—' she stammered helplessly, unable to

find the words to express her consternation, and
with a shake of his head he had pulled her closer
to him and bent his mouth to hers.

She thought at first he had intended to kiss
her as a form of punishment, a way of avenging
himself for her embarrassing departure from the
club, but it didn't work out that way at all. From
the minute his lips touched hers everything
changed, and what had begun as a tentative caress
deepened into a passionate embrace. The fact that
they were standing in a street—albeit a quiet
one—in broad daylight, meant nothing to Tobie.
She had lost all sense of time and consequence,
and when he finally lifted his head she was weak
with emotion.

'Come on,' he had said, in a husky voice, urging her forward along the pavement, and she went
with him, making no objection when they came
to where a low steel-grey sports car was parked,
and he put her into the front seat, before striding
round the bonnet to get in beside her. . .

'Can't you sleep?'

Mark's concerned voice broke into her reverie,
and she turned almost guiltily to find him behind
her. She had been so far from this colourful little
island that it was incredibly difficult to reorientate
herself. She stared at him blankly for several
seconds before recovering her composure, and
was grateful for his obtuseness when he added
gently:

'It's the jet lag, isn't it? It takes some getting
used to. You're tired, but you feel you shouldn't
be, isn't that right? It's a kind of mental hurdle,

and it affects different people different ways. Personally, I find the atmosphere here makes me feel rather sleepy, and I never have any trouble adjusting to the time change.'

Tobie bent her head. 'How lucky for you,' she commented, and fortunately Mark didn't hear the irony in her tone. Nevertheless, the fact that it was there at all troubled her, and she felt the start of a headache hammering at her temples. It was the thought of tomorrow, she realised uneasily, the thought of going to Emerald Cay and meeting Robert again, with the awareness of his condition like a Damoclean sword hanging over her head.

'We could make love,' Mark murmured now, sliding his arms about her waist and drawing her closer to him, but as usual, Tobie panicked at the possessive touch of his hands. There were times, like this, when she wondered if she would be able to respond to any man again, and her words were sharper than they might have been because of her uncertainty.

'Oh, not now, Mark!' she exclaimed, releasing herself without consideration for his feelings, her sense of guilt redoubling at the awareness of the pain she was inflicting. 'I—want to take a shower, and get changed for dinner. Do you mind?'

Mark hesitated. 'Is something wrong?' he asked perceptively, alerted by her nervousness, and with a sigh she spread her hands.

'I've got a headache, if you must know,' she admitted unwillingly. 'I—I've had it since we got off the plane. I'm sorry if I'm bad company, but it really is painful.'

'Hey, why didn't you say?' Mark disappeared back into his own room to reappear a few moments later with a bottle of tablets. 'Here, swallow a couple of these. They'll take care of the headache, and the jet lag. Take a cool shower, and I'll meet you in the bar downstairs in half an hour. I promise you, you'll feel a different woman.'

Tobie wished she could feel as sure, but she thanked him for his kindness, bestowing a warm kiss of appeasement on his mouth before he departed once more. 'I don't deserve you, do you know that?' she murmured, touching his cheek with wondering fingers, and he captured them and carried them to his mouth before wishing her a gruff farewell.

The twin-engined Cessna made its approach to the tiny airstrip on Emerald Cay at eleven o'clock the following morning. As it circled the small island, Mark pointed out the places of interest to Tobie, leaning past her to indicate the whereabouts of his brother's villa, and to share her admiration of the shimmering green waters of the lagoon.

'The reef provides a natural barrier to intruders,' he remarked, drawing her attention to its exposed teeth. 'There's one point of access, below the villa. Rob had an entry blasted in the coral so that his yacht can get in and out, but otherwise. . .' He shrugged.

Tobie digested this. So Robert had a yacht. It was probably one of those motor yachts, the luxurious kind she had seen in the harbour at Castries that morning, not one of the tall-masted sailing vessels, whose sails looked so picturesque against the azure blue waters of the ocean. Robert had always loved speed, and Mark had told her that some of them could do thirty knots.

'How many people live on the island?' she asked now, trying to compose herself for their arrival, and Mark frowned.

'Let me see—well, there's Monique and Henri. They're the married couple who look after the villa. Monique does most of the cooking and cleaning, and Henri looks after the garden. My mother instructs them, of course. She's Rob's housekeeper.'

'I see.' Tobie digested this. 'And—and that's all?'

'No. There are one or two of Monique and Henri's offspring about the place. I think their eldest son is married, and he and his wife live down near the harbour and look after the boats. Then there's Harvey Jennings, of course. He and his daughter live on the far side of the island. Rob bought the place from them, and he lets them stay here free gratis.'

Tobie glanced at him. 'You don't like them?' she asked, responding to the censure in his voice, and Mark shrugged again.

'I don't like Harvey,' he admitted. 'He's a sponger, always making out he's hard up. He relies on Rob far too much. Cilla—well, she's all right. Quite a nice girl, actually. She's often at the villa. My mother likes her too. I know that Cilla comes over for different reasons, but there you are. Rob's a likeable character.'

He shrugged, but it wasn't difficult to understand his meaning, and Tobie was appalled by her own reactions to it. Even after all this time, she could still feel the agony of Robert's desertion, and she doubted coming here was going to blunt the pain.

The aircraft landed, and Mark went to bid farewell to their pilot. He had introduced him to Tobie as Jim Matheson, and as they crossed the airstrip he explained that Robert and the pilot owned the plane jointly.

'It's a small business venture,' he remarked, glancing back at the blue and white Cessna glinting in the sunlight. 'They own half a dozen of these small aircraft, hiring them out for trips around the islands. You'd be surprised how many people enjoy island-hopping, as they call it. It's quite a going concern.'

Tobie was impressed, or at least she hoped she appeared that way. Inside, she was a churning mass of tangled emotions, and the sight of the gleaming convertible, parked in the shade of a clump of palm trees, obviously waiting for them, filled her with real panic.

'*Mark!*'

The affectionate calling of his name, accompanied by the sight of an elegant woman in her late fifties climbing out of the back of the vehicle, told its own story. Evidently, this was his mother, come to meet them, and Tobie breathed a little easier when she saw that the only other occupant of the car was black.

Mark allowed himself to be enveloped in a warm embrace, and over his shoulder Tobie met the strangely malevolent eyes of the woman who had deserted her eldest son when he was little more than seven years old. She had left her home, and her family, to run away with a man more than twice her age, and that was what had created the rift between her and Robert, the rift Tobie had never expected to see mended. Mark was her second husband's son, of course, but his father was dead now. Mark had told her he had died of a heart attack soon after Marks's eighteenth birthday, and it was this as much as anything which had turned his interest towards medicine. Robert's own father had committed suicide. A week after the divorce was made absolute he had hanged himself in the summerhouse of their Kingston home, and Robert had been brought up by a series of nannies, acting under his aunt's instructions. His own mother had made little effort to see him, too absorbed with her new life and her new baby, and it was only when Robert became famous that he began getting letters from her. Letters he had destroyed, so far as Tobie was aware—until the accident—

Standing there with the sun beating down upon her head, Tobie tried desperately to relax. She was here now. There was nothing she could do about it. And if Robert's mother knew who she was, and that was why she was looking at her so hostilely, there was nothing she could do about that either. Perhaps Mrs Newman was merely jealous of her younger son's affection. But if there was any other reason for her hostility, she would soon find out.

Mark was freeing himself from his mother's embrace now, assuring her that they had had a good journey—that he was in the best of health—that he wasn't working too hard—and that no, he hadn't lost weight. He was obviously amused by his mother's insistence, but as Tobie waited somewhat apprehensively to be introduced, she had the feeling that Mrs Newman's delaying tactics were deliberate.

At last Mark succeeded in drawing her forward, and with evident pride he introduced her to his mother. 'Isn't she lovely?' he demanded, his arm possessively about Tobie's shoulders. 'I told you she was. Don't you think I'm the luckiest man in the world?'

His mother viewed Tobie with cool assessing eyes. She was a tall woman, like her son, almost as tall as Tobie's five feet six inches, with the heavier limbs of middle age. Yet she was quite an attractive woman still, with greying blonde hair and fair skin, that just avoided the gnarled weathered look. If she had had any heartache in her life she disguised it well, and presented the appearance of someone well able to take care of herself. She seemed much more Mark's mother than Robert's, and only the inimical gaze of her dark brown eyes reminded Tobie of how Robert had looked when he slammed out of the apartment that fatal afternoon.

'So nice to meet you—er—Tobie,' she said now, offering a curiously limp hand, and Tobie took it.

'It was kind of you to invite me,' she said, forcing a tight smile. 'You live in a very beautiful part of the world.'

'Oh, you must thank my son for your invitation,' Mrs Newman demurred, her remark verging on discourtesy, and Tobie stiffened.

'I've thanked Mark, naturally,' she said, glancing at him, but his mother quickly intervened.

'I meant Robert, of course,' she said, ignoring her younger son's discomfort. 'Emerald Cay belongs to him, not to us, and it was he who offered the invitation.'

It was a body blow, but whether Mrs Newman was aware of its significance, Tobie could not be sure. After all, if Robert had not told her about their relationship, how could she know? And yet there was something here, some undercurrent that Tobie sensed but could not make contact with.

'Well, we're here, anyway,' Mark observed tautly, his expression mirroring his impatience with his mother. 'So let's go, shall we? It's hot, and I for one could do with a dip in the pool.'

'Of course. I'm sorry.'

Tobie guessed Mrs Newman really meant it as she gestured towards the car. She was obviously very fond of Mark, but in spite of her comments about Robert, Tobie wasn't altogether sure how she felt towards him. Yet they must be friends. They lived here together. They shared the same house. There had to be some feeling between them.

The drive from the airstrip to the villa gave her a little time to assimilate her own position. The news that Robert had offered the invitation required some adjustment in her thinking, and she couldn't help wondering how he proposed to behave towards her. She had thought if he hadn't admitted to Mark that he knew her before, he could be relied upon not to do so now, but that was not taking into account his condition, and who knew what quirks in his personality that might have created? She was both apprehensive and uneasy, and her feelings made a mockery of her boast to Laura that she loved Mark, and nothing Robert did could change that.

The road curved up from the flat stretch of earth that provided a landing strip, climbing towards the hills that formed the backbone of the island. It was a dusty track, rutted in places, where the rains had dislodged the stones that held the track together, but the scenery was so magnificent one could ignore the discomfort.

As they climbed, beyond the airstrip they could see miles and miles of unbroken sand, stretching to infinity. This side of the island must be unin-habited, Tobie thought, and the lace-edged waters of the ocean were the only intruders on these shores. It was a disturbing concept, and she experienced a moment's awareness of how shipwrecked mariners must have felt when faced with their own insignificance.

The hillside was thickly covered with stunted trees and flowering shrubs, their roots even encroaching on to the road at times. One could stretch out one's hand and touch them as one passed, and Mark snatched a magnolia blossom to tuck behind Tobie's ear. She shared his laughter for a moment, and then encountering his mother's speculative gaze was silenced.

As if sensing the sudden tension, Mark broke into conversation, asking how Robert was, questioning his mother about his brother's paralysis.

Mrs Newman seemed unnecessarily pessimistic about her son's condition. 'He says he's quite well,' she replied, plucking at the leather on the back of the seat in front. 'But you know how independent he is. I keep my own counsel. I have my own opinion. I know what his doctors say. But it's not a subject I'd advise you to discuss with him. At least—' she paused, allowing her eyes to move to Tobie once more, 'not in front of—strangers.'

'But he's—no worse?' Mark insisted, his hand finding Tobie's in gentle reassurance, and his mother shrugged.

'Were it not for the lingering amnesia, I'd say he is as recovered as he'll ever be,' she responded succinctly, and when Tobie's head jerked towards her, a mocking smile tugged at the corners of her mouth. 'Didn't Mark tell you, my dear?' she enquired, with what Tobie was almost convinced was malicious amusement. 'Robert still suffers a mental blackout of everything that happened immediately before the accident. He's lost six whole months of his life. Isn't that a shame?'

CHAPTER TWO

ROBERT's villa lay on the south-west side of the island, above the tiny manmade harbour. As they came down the winding road towards the sea again, Tobie saw its sprawling green-tiled roof, and realised it was much more than the comfortably-sized bungalow she had envisaged. It was much bigger, for one thing, and set on different levels, it looked more like a Spanish hacienda, with the large circular swimming pool providing a focal point. The walls were colour-washed in pastel shades, and overgrown with clinging vines and bougainvillaea, and as they drew nearer she could see the white shutters bolted back against the walls, and the arched courtyard below the patio. It was, without doubt, the most beautiful house she had ever seen, and in other circumstances she would hardly have been able to contain her excitement. As it was, she felt a bewildered sense of confusion, and was troubled by the knowledge that Mark's mother was not as ingenuous as he imagined her to be.

As the sleek convertible entered the tiled courtyard, Mark pointed down to the harbour below them, where a tall-masted sloop lay at anchor. 'The *Ariadne*,' he told her whimsically. 'Beautiful, isn't she?'

'Th-that's Robert's yacht?' Tobie ventured.

29

'The same,' agreed Mark lightly. 'Fancy a sail?'

'Per-perhaps.' The car had come to a halt, and Tobie avoided his mother's eyes as she climbed out. 'I—it's not what I expected.'

'What did you expect, Miss Kennedy?' enquired a low voice from somewhere behind her, and her whole body froze in an attitude of consternation. 'Some kind of motor launch, perhaps? Something I can control with my hands? Or am I being unkind, and you didn't mean to be tactless?'

'Rob!'

Mark's ejaculation was both impatient and enthusiastic. Turning quickly to face the man whose wheelchair had rolled so silently up behind them, he shook his hand energetically, unknowingly giving Tobie time to gather her scattered senses. He obviously shared her disconcertion at his brother's unexpected appearance, but he could have no idea of the traumatic effect Robert's arrival had had on her. She had expected to be shocked, she had expected some kind of physical reaction; but nothing had prepared her for the emotions that swept so devastatingly through her as she encountered those achingly familiar features.

He hadn't changed, or at least, not a lot. He was thinner, perhaps, and there were streaks of grey in the night-dark hair that brushed the collar of his open-necked denim shirt, but he still possessed those disturbingly uneven features that combined to make such an attractive whole. He was looking at her now in frank appraisal, but there was no element of recognition in that coolly admiring glance. He was looking at her as a man might look at the girl his brother was expected to marry, and she knew with a wrench that that was the cruellest cut of all.

Her eyes dropped lower, over the long legs, folded on to the chair's footrest, jean-clad and casual, but without the strength they had had when he first walked into the gallery less than four years ago, and she knew a pain like nothing she had ever known before. *Oh, God!* she thought in agony, *I did this to him! And he doesn't even know me!*

'Let me introduce you,' Mark was saying now, shaking his head over Robert's unconventional method of greeting his guests. 'This, as you've already divined, is Tobie. Tobie, allow me to introduce you to your favourite artist— Robert Lang!'

'Painter, Mark,' Robert inserted dryly, holding out his hand towards her in apparent friendliness. 'How do you do, Miss Kennedy? You'll have to forgive my not getting up. It's not so easy as it used to be.'

'How—how do you do?'

Somehow Tobie articulated the words, withdrawing her hand as swiftly as possible from the firm coolness of his. Hers felt hot and sticky, and even that slight contact had left her feeling weak and shaken.

'Call her Tobie,' Mark intervened, putting a possessive hand on her shoulder. 'She's going to be your sister-in-law, Rob. Don't you approve?'

'Very much.' Robert was polite. 'And a fan, no less. Tell me, Miss—I mean, Tobie—are you an expert?'

Tobie swallowed with difficulty before replying. 'I—I just know what I like,' she said, giving the stock answer, and Mrs Newman moved forward authoritatively to take charge of Robert's chair.

'Come along,' she said. 'I think we could all do with a drink, don't you? Henri, ask Monique to fetch some iced lime juice to the patio, and tell her we'll eat in an hour.'

'Yes, m'm,' responded the black man, who had chauffeured the car from the landing strip and was presently unloading their cases on to the courtyard, but as Mrs Newman attempted to wheel his chair forward, Robert dislodged her fingers with an impatient gesture. It was the first sign he had shown of any irritation with his condition, and Tobie intercepted the sympathetic glance that Mark and his mother exchanged. Curiously enough, their attitude irritated her, too, and she was not surprised when Robert countermanded his mother's instructions.

'You can wheel me up to the verandah first, Henri,' he said, his tone brooking no argument. 'I've already asked Monique to provide refreshments, so you can attend to the luggage.'

'Yes, sir.' Henri's dark face creased into a smile, but Mrs Newman's expression was less easy to read as they all began to move towards the house.

There was a slope beside the steps that ran up from the courtyard to the patio above, and although Robert's electric chair could come down in safety, he needed assistance to reach the upper level. Following behind, Tobie felt her nails digging into her palms as she climbed the short flight of steps, and then anxiety was suspended as she had her first real sight of the villa and its surroundings.

The house itself was built on Spanish lines, as she had first suspected, with low-hanging eaves, and grilled balconies, and a winding iron staircase, attached to the main building, giving access to an upper floor. The various levels of the house ran out in different directions, and all the rooms had long windows, opened wide to the sun, and the salt-scented breeze that dispelled the humidity. In front of the villa lustrous Italian tiles surrounded the poolside area, with wooden *cabañas* set among vinecoloured trellises providing changing rooms. It was even bigger at close range than she had anticipated, and she became aware that Robert was watching her and her reactions to it.

'Welcome to Soledad,' he said, with wry humour, as Henri was dismissed, and he propelled himself across the sun-dappled patio. 'What do you think of my house—Tobie? Would you say it was wasted on a cripple like me?'

'Rob!'

'Robert!'

Mark and his mother spoke simultaneously, but Tobie knew he expected her to answer. It was a natural question, after all, albeit an uncomfortably candid one, and Mark had warned her of his sarcasm.

'I don't think you believe you're a cripple, Mr Lang, any more than I do,' she ventured carefully. 'And no one who appreciates beauty as you do should be denied such magnificent surroundings.'

'You know I appreciate beauty?' he mused. 'How would you know a thing like that?'

Tobie's cheeks burned. 'I know your work, Mr Lang,' she defended herself quickly. 'M——Mark told you, I admire it very much.'

Robert brought his chair to a halt in the shade of the balcony where a glass-topped table was set with a jug of iced fruit juice, several frosted glasses, and a bottle of champagne in an ice-bucket. He indicated that they should make themselves comfortable on the cushioned basket-weave chairs nearby, and then himself took charge of the champagne, uncorking it easily, and allowing the bubbling overflow to spill carelessly on to the tiles.

'You'll all join me, I hope,' he said, reaching for one of the tall narrow glasses and filling it. 'I think a toast is in order, don't you?' He passed the glass to Tobie, and then filling another handed it to his mother. 'To the good times, hmm? For all of us? But most especially to Mark and Tobie. Good luck!'

Tobie sipped the delicately flavoured liquid with trembling lips. This was all wrong, she thought unhappily. This wasn't at all the way she had expected it to be. But why, when everything seemed so normal, did she feel so uneasy?

In spite of her apprehension, no one else seemed perturbed by the situation, and although she contributed little to it, conversation became general. Mark asked Robert about his painting, and Robert, in his turn, questioned his brother about his work at the hospital. They were obviously good friends, and under cover of their discussion Mrs Newman suggested that Tobie might like to see her room. It was a polite suggestion, and Tobie had no reason to object to it, and yet she was curiously reluctant to find herself alone with Mark's mother.

However, Mark had overheard and he seconded his mother's proposal, nodding his head and adding lazily: 'Put your swimsuit on, honey. We don't stand on ceremony here, and I intend to show you how fit I am, in spite of just surviving an English winter.'

Tobie managed a slight smile, and then rose to accompany the older woman into the house. Her last image was of Robert's face turned politely in her direction, with just the faintest hint of a frown drawing his brows together.

They entered the house by means of a garden room, where flowering plants and shrubs filled the air with their exotic perfume. All thresholds had been moulded to allow the free passage of Robert's wheelchair, Tobie noticed, and she wondered who looked after him. Someone must help him to bathe and dress, but so far as she could see, there were only the two servants.

'Robert's rooms are downstairs, naturally,'

Mrs Newman observed now, as they entered an almost circular entrance hall, with a magnificent chandelier hanging at the foot of a curving flight of stairs. 'This is the oldest part of the house, but as you probably noticed, there have been various additions made in recent years.'

'It's—beautiful,' said Tobie helplessly, unable to think of anything else to say, and after a moment's hesitation, Mark's mother led the way up the stairs.

At the top of the stairs, a balcony circled the hall below, with corridors leading off in several directions. Their complexity made Tobie believe that she would never be able to find her way about, and after following Mrs Newman along one of them, up and down odd little staircases set into the hillside, she was convinced of it.

Nevertheless, when they reached the suite of rooms assigned to her for her stay, her gratitude was such that she forgot her earlier antipathy.

An arched doorway led into a spacious sleeping apartment overlooking the sweep of the headland and the ocean beyond. French doors opened on to a corner balcony, private from the rest of the house, with an unlimited vista of the terraced gardens that fell away below the villa. The room itself was furnished in shades of cream and turquoise, with a heavily embossed cream quilt on the wide bed and long turquoise silk curtains at the windows. Adjoining this room was a small dressing room, and beyond that a luxurious bathroom, in matching pastel shades.

'I don't know what to say,' Tobie murmured.

'It's just—perfect.' She fingered a label hanging from the handle of one of her suitcases, which had been set on an ottoman at the foot of the bed. 'Thank you so much.'

Mrs Newman paused in the doorway. 'Don't thank me,' she responded tersely. 'As I said before, this is Robert's house, not mine.'

She would have gone then, but Tobie knew she had to say something. 'You—you don't want me here, Mrs Newman?' she queried cautiously. 'You—have some objection to my—friendship with Mark?'

'Did I say so?' The older woman's eyes were wary.

'No, but—'

'So long as both my sons are happy, I'm content,' Mrs Newman replied smoothly, and without giving Tobie a chance to say anything more, she left her.

It would take too long to unpack all her clothes, so Tobie contented herself with unlocking the cases and taking out the most crushable items. Then, stripping off the skirt and cotton shirt she had worn to travel in, she rummaged around for her swimsuits. She had brought three bikinis—a white one, with black edging, a yellow one, which she knew toned well with her creamy skin, and a dark brown one, with red beading, that was without doubt the most provocative of them all. Mark had asked her to put her swimsuit on, and she had no doubt he meant what he said, but looking at their skimpy appearance, she was curiously unwilling to expose herself before Robert

in one of them. Before she had known of his
accident she had intended to do so deliberately,
but now—now she felt quite different, knowing
he could not join them.

Running distraught hands through the silky
weight of her hair, she caught a glimpse of herself
in the long mirrors attached to the vanity unit,
and on impulse she turned to face herself fully.
In nothing but flimsy bikini briefs she studied
her reflection critically, wondering whether, had
Robert not suffered the amnesia, he would see
any great change in her. She was older, of course,
three years older, with the memory of her experi-
ences adding a touch of mystery to eyes he had
always found fascinating. Green eyes, they were,
with long curling lashes, her best feature, she had
maintained, in spite of Robert's assertion that she
had more desirable attributes. Certainly her figure
was good, with full, rounded breasts, and a narrow waist above the swell of her hips. Her legs
were long, slim, without being angular, and she
had lived long enough to know that she had that
indefinable something that men found attractive.
Did Robert find her attractive now? she wondered, despising herself for the traitorous thought,
but unable to prevent it. If she had met him as she
had done before, without ties or complications,
would he still have found her desirable? It was a
tantalising idea, but one which she recognised as
being the most dangerous notion she had had
since first she learned of Mark's identity.

In the event, she decided to wear the yellow
bikini, teaming it with a wrap-around cotton skirt

patterned in shades of brown and white. It left her legs and shoulders bare, but it was at least as concealing as a sundress, and she could easily shed the skirt when she had to.

Finding her way back to the patio was not as difficult as she had at first imagined. There were plenty of windows along the winding passages to keep her in touch with her whereabouts, and she emerged on to the balcony above the hall with a feeling of achievement.

To her relief, Mark was just mounting the stairs as she went to go down, and she waited at the top for him to join her. 'Do I look all right?' she whispered protestingly, as he reached for her, but his murmur of approval was muffled against the satiny skin of her shoulder.

'Go and talk to my brother,' he said huskily, when at last he let her go. 'I won't begrudge him a few minutes of your company. But remember, I saw you first, hmm?'

Tobie's tongue circled her lips. 'I—I'll wait for you,' she demurred, reluctant to leave the safety of his presence, but he urged her forward.

'I shan't be long,' he promised, bestowing a last kiss on her parted lips. 'And knowing you're with Rob, I'll make sure I don't waste time.'

Tobie's smile was uncertain, but she had no reason not to do as he asked, and besides, why should she feel so anxious? Robert had not recognised her. So far as he was concerned, she was his brother's girl-friend, and nothing else. If all went well, she could leave here without even ruffling the surface of her relationship with

Mark, and surely that was what she wanted.

Taking a deep breath, she descended the stairs, and walked briskly across the hall and out through the garden room. The gurgling fountain that kept the plants watered had a cooling sound, and she tried to emulate its unhurried progress.

Outside, the sun seemed more brilliant, and she wished she had thought to bring her dark glasses with her. Their shade would have provided anonymity as well as protection against the glare, but aware that Robert had observed her appearance, she could hardly turn and march back into the house again. Instead, she compelled herself to put one sandalled foot in front of the other, crossing the tiles to where his chair was situated with what she hoped appeared to be calm composure.

He was alone. No doubt Mrs Newman was attending to her duties as housekeeper and supervising the arrangements for lunch, but Robert remained much where they had left him, staring thoughtfully out across the sparkling green waters of the pool. There was a moment, before he turned to greet her, when Tobie could watch him unobserved, and her heart lurched at the remembrance of what they had once shared. It was almost impossible, seeing him sitting there so casually, so *relaxed*, to imagine he was incapable of getting up out of his chair, and she hardly understood the emotions that gripped her at that awareness. There was pity, of course, and sympathy, too, despite Mark's assertion to her that Robert would welcome neither, but it wasn't only compassion that brought such an unwilling sense of awareness. They had been too close to dismiss their relationship lightly. They had loved, they had been *lovers*. And for the first time, she could think of the past without so much bitterness.

'Tobie!' He had observed her approach and now hailed her with friendly enthusiasm. 'Come and join me. Mark's gone to get changed, but I don't suppose he'll be long.'

'No—no. I—I saw him.' Tobie automatically quickened her step and came to stand beside him. 'I—er—isn't this a marvellous view?' She gestured towards the harbour and the wide expanse of ocean beyond. 'I should think you never get tired of looking at it.'

'You'd be surprised,' he remarked dryly, glancing up at her with wry humour. 'When it's the only view you see, it can become a little—monotonous.'

'Oh, I —' Tobie flushed. 'I didn't mean—that is—I didn't intend to imply—'

'I know.' His smile was heartbreakingly familiar. 'So—won't you sit down? Or must I get a crick in my neck looking up at you?'

'I'm sorry.' Tobie bumped down jerkily on to the low lounger beside him. 'I didn't think.' Her fingers closed over the rim of the cushion she was sitting on. 'Er—it's a beautiful day, isn't it? It was raining when we left London.'

'Was it?' Now his eyes were slightly above hers. 'Yes, that's one thing you can be sure of here. We usually have beautiful days.'

She sensed the irony in his tones and realised

she was not making a good job of this. He probably thought she was one of those useless
females, without a thought in their heads outside
of the latest fashions and make-up, and certainly
she had not displayed any particular intelligence
in their conversation so far.

'Do—er—do you work indoors, Mr Lang?'
she ventured now, choosing the subject least
likely to prove controversial, and he inclined
his head.

'In a manner of speaking,' he agreed, half turning in his seat to indicate a path that led around
the side of the building. 'I have a studio that's
attached to the house, but only accessible from
the outside, if you know what I mean. It's along
there, if you're interested. And the name is
Robert, Tobie. I can't have my future sister-in-
law calling me *Mr* Lang.'

Tobie's colour deepened again. 'Very well,'
she murmured awkwardly. 'I—are you working
at the moment?'

'At this moment?' he asked provokingly, the
dark eyes full of amusement, and Tobie sighed.

'You know what I mean,' she exclaimed,
speaking without thinking for the first time.
'I mean, have you a commission at present? I
don't suppose there's much scope for portrait
painting here.'

'You sound very knowledgeable,' he remarked,
his dark eyes narrowing. 'Do you know much
about painting, Tobie? And don't tell me again
that you know what you like.'

This was deeper water, and Tobie immediately

sought for the shallows. 'I—I used to work in an art gallery once,' she said, and instantly regretted the admission. Mark didn't even know that, and by confessing such a thing to Robert she was stepping dangerously near disaster.

'An art gallery,' he murmured now, his eyes watching her closely. 'What art gallery? Where? In London?'

'I—in Reading, actually,' she lied, saying the name of the first town that came into her head. 'It was just a small place. Not a proper art gallery really, a sort of—adjunct to the—to the public library.'

Robert frowned. 'Really?'

She nodded. 'But—but I gave that up a long time ago. I work for an insurance company now, in Holborn. Do you know Holborn, Mr Lang?'

'Robert,' he amended dryly, and then shrugged. 'I used to know London very well. I used to live there. But since my accident. . .'

'. . .you've lived here,' Tobie finished for him eager to change the subject. 'You're very lucky really, being able to escape to such an island paradise.'

'Is that how you see it?' Robert enquired with a grimace. 'It's a lonely life, Tobie. Lonely, and—unfulfilled.'

Tobie bent her head, feeling the heat of the sun burning her shoulders. 'I should have thought your work was—fulfilling,' she commented, feeling obliged to say something, as he made a sound of exasperation.

'I'm sure my mother thinks so, too,' he essayed

wryly, reaching for the almost empty bottle of champagne, residing in the melted ice cubes. 'Will you join me?' and when she shook her head, he poured the remainder into his glass and surveyed it with a crooked smile. 'She doesn't understand, I was a man first and painter second. I think she expects those roles to be reversed.'

Tobie darted a look up at him. 'And they're not?' she asked involuntarily, almost immediately realising the antagonism she had provoked.

'What do you think that crash did to me, Tobie?' he demanded harshly. 'It didn't paralyse my feelings—my *emotions*! They still function as they always did.'

'I—I'm sorry.' Tobie was horrified at her blunder. 'I didn't—I didn't mean—'

The sound of footsteps ringing across the stone tiles stilled her fumbling apology, and she sat there in mortified silence as Mark threw his towel down on to a lounger and stretched with evident self-satisfaction.

'Magic,' he remarked, half to himself, and then turned to his half-brother and Tobie. 'So—how goes it? You two seemed deep in conversation when I came out of the house. What have you been telling her about me, Rob? Do I detect a certain aloofness in the air?'

'Don't be silly, Mark.'

Tobie got hastily to her feet, and as she did so Robert said indolently: 'Don't be so conceited, little brother. Your name hasn't even been mentioned.'

'No?' Mark pretended to be put out. 'Hey,

Tobie, what's been going on? Has he been taking liberties behind my back?'

'I—no, of course not.' Tobie found she couldn't joke about it, and it was left to Robert to make light of their conversation.

'We've been discussing my work, actually,' he admitted at last. 'You know what an egoist I am. I can't resist extolling my talents to a willing listener.'

Mark grimaced. 'I'll believe you,' he conceded good-naturedly. 'But only because I know it's true.' He turned to Tobie. 'So come on. I'll race you round the pool, and if you win I'll let you duck me, so long as I'm given the same privilege.'

Tobie hesitated. 'It's nearly lunchtime,' she demurred, in no mood to act the fool with him, but Mark was adamant.

'Lunch can wait,' he said, advancing on her with menacing steps. 'Now do you go quietly, or do I have to use force?'

Tobie backed away from him helplessly, realising she had to go through with this. But as she dropped her skirt and turned to dive smoothly into the water, it was Robert's expression she remembered.

CHAPTER THREE

To her relief, Robert made no further mention of the conversation they had had. The things she had admitted to him and the embarrassing remark she had made were all forgotten, and the rest of the day passed without incident. During the afternoon, while Robert rested, Mark took her on a tour of the island in a multi-coloured beach buggy, which he said Henri used to bring supplies up from the harbour, and after dinner she was much too tired to want to linger long on the terrace. She said goodnight, and made her way to her room, falling asleep almost as soon as her head touched the pillow.

The following morning, however, she awakened extremely early. With her body still attuned to European time, she was out of bed before six o'clock, stepping on to her balcony, shivering in the unexpected coolness of the salt-laden breeze. But it was deliciously refreshing, and she wondered if Mark was awake, and as eager to explore as she was.

On impulse, she shrugged off the shred of cambric she had worn to sleep in, and after sluicing her face and cleaning her teeth, she got dressed. She wore her bathing suit, because she had every intention of using the pool, but she pulled on a pair of baggy cotton pants over the

black and white bikini, amazed to see that already
her day in the sun had left the faint marks of
her bra straps over her shoulders. With her hair
confined by a black velvet hair ribbon, she left
her room, threading her way along the corridors
on impatient feet.

No one seemed to be about, and she wondered
what time Monique served breakfast. Dinner had
been served by candlelight the night before. They
had eaten at the long dining table, overlooking
the floodlit waters of the pool, and Tobie had
found the effect quite intoxicating. The men had
worn dinner jackets, or at least Mark had, his
brother's wine-coloured velvet jacket serving him
equally elegantly. Robert had presided at the head
of the table, with his mother on his right and
Tobie on his left, but as Mark had monopolised
the conversation, she had had little chance to
amend the opinion he must now have of her.
Perhaps today she would be able to repair her
image, although why it was so important that she
should do so, she didn't care to analyse.

Mark had given her a short tour of the downstairs rooms before dinner, and now she knew
where the living and eating rooms were, and the
ways to get in and out of the villa. Most of the
downstairs rooms had French doors anyway, but
as well as these, there was a front and a back
entrance through elegantly arched portals.

Now, realising that the villa was probably still
locked for the night, Tobie made her way to the
garden room, deciding it would be easier to open
the windows than the doors. But to her surprise,

the windows of the garden room stood wide, their wild silk curtains fluttering in the errant breeze, and from the pool came the distinct sound of splashing water.

So Mark was up after all. With lightening spirits, Tobie stepped out on to the patio, sauntering across the mosaic tiling that surrounded the pool. She could see a dark head under the water, swimming strongly across the pool, and kicking off her sandals, she rolled up the legs of her pants and squatted down on the rim of the basin, dipping her toes into the water.

The swimmer surfaced just below where she was sitting, but her anticipated words of teasing admiration died on her tongue. It was not Mark's square-cut shoulders that emerged from the water, but Robert's lean dark features, one hand raised to push back the dripping wetness of his hair. She didn't know which of them was the most surprised, but one thing was certain, Robert was the first to recover.

'Tobie,' he greeted her politely, keeping himself afloat without apparent effort. 'Did you sleep well?'

'Oh—yes, thank you.' Tobie caught her lower lip between her teeth. 'The—er—the water feels cold.'

'Not to me,' he remarked tautly. 'Did you come to swim?'

Tobie shrugged. 'I thought I might.' She sighed. 'But if I'm intruding—'

'Not at all.' He granted her a faint smile. 'If you'll give me a few minutes to get out—'

'Is that necessary?' Tobie broke into his speech. 'I mean——' she made an awkward gesture, 'I won't get in your way.'

'But I might get in yours,' he retorted flatly. 'Do you mind? I am rather sensitive about being observed. If you'll just hand me that robe. . .' He gestured to a navy towelling gown that was draped over the nearby lounger. 'I'll only be a few minutes.'

Tobie drew her knees up to her chin, preparatory to getting to her feet, and then allowed them to drop down again. 'Robert, really. . .' she began, using his name without really thinking about it. 'Please don't leave on my account. I——I'll go, if you want. I——I didn't intend to interrupt your swim. Please——just go on as if I wasn't here.'

Robert's firm mouth twisted. 'Do you think that's possible?' he enquired dryly, his expression softening slightly. 'Somehow I don't think Mark would agree with you.'

'Mark's not here,' she retorted simply, and then wished she hadn't when Robert's expression hardened again.

'No, he's not,' he agreed shortly. 'But I'm telling you, he wouldn't like it. Now, be a good girl and get my robe, hmm?'

Tobie hesitated. 'As a matter of fact, I'm glad I've met you like this,' she said, after a moment. 'I——I wanted to apologise. About yesterday. I—— I didn't mean what I said to sound the way it did.'

'It doesn't matter.' Robert swam to the side, and draped his arms over the rim. 'Now, do you mind? I'm getting cold.'

'Oh! Oh, of course.'

Tobie scrambled to her feet then, retrieving the robe and bringing it back to the shallow steps she could now see below the level of the water.

'Let me help you,' she said unthinkingly, and saw the darkening anger in his eyes.

'I can manage,' he insisted, dragging the robe out of her hands and tossing it down on to the side of the pool. 'Go away, Tobie. Let me do this my way. I don't need your assistance.'

She sighed, still lingering. 'I'm not squeamish, you know,' she ventured. 'I'd like to help you. Where's your chair? Let me get it for you.' She looked round, her brow furrowing. 'Where is it?'

'Go away, Tobie!' There was real anger in his voice now, and she looked down at him frustratedly.

'Why won't you let me help you? Why won't you tell me where your chair is? How did you get here?'

With a groan of exasperation he rested his forehead on the rim of the pool, and then said in a muffled tone: 'I walked here. On sticks. Didn't Mark tell you about those? I'm sure he must have done. Mark's very meticulous about my condition.'

Tobie remembered now. 'He—he did say something,' she admitted in a low voice. 'I—er—I'll go and take a shower. I'll see you later—'

'No, wait!' Now it was Robert who detained her, hauling himself up on to the side of the pool and sitting there as she had done, with his feet in the water. She was surprised to see that in spite

of his debility, his body and legs were deeply
tanned, and she guessed that he spent long hours
in the sun. His only attire was the sawn-off denim
shorts he had worn to swim in, their frayed edges
drawing her attention to the muscled strength of
his thighs.

'Look,' he said quietly, 'I'd rather you didn't
tell Mark you'd found me here.' He hunched his
shoulders, exposing the white bones under the
skin of his back. There was not an ounce of spare
flesh on him, and she wondered, with a ridiculous
sense of responsibility, whether he was eating
enough. 'He doesn't—that is, I'd rather he didn't
know about this until I'm more—proficient. Do
you know what I'm saying?'

'I think so.' Tobie nodded. 'You mean that
Mark doesn't know you use the pool.'

'Something like that,' Robert agreed, resting
his chin on his chest. 'Do you mind?'

Tobie shook her head. 'Of course not. If you'd
rather I didn't.'

'I would,' he affirmed, looking quizzically up
at her again. 'Don't look so worried. I'm not
planning to drown myself.'

'I—I never thought you were,' she stammered, aware that his words had reminded her
disturbingly of his father's abrupt demise, and
he grinned suddenly.

'Okay. It's our secret, hmm?' He glanced
behind him, reaching for the bathrobe. 'And
now. . .'

'You want me to go?'

His eyes narrowed, dropping down over the

swell of her breasts to the band of bare midriff
displayed between the hem of her bra and the belt
of her pants. Then, abruptly, they returned to her
face again, and she was left in little doubt that
he considered the remark provocative.

'Yes, I want you to go,' he said, with an edge
to his voice, and she turned to make good her
escape.

But she had forgotten the pool behind her, and
instead of encountering the firm surface of the
tiles, she found herself treading air. Her gulp of
surprise was quickly stifled by the salt water, and
she sank chokingly beneath the surface as the
weight of her pants dragged her down.

Panic flared, and she was clawing for the air
again when firm hands gripped her, assisting her
progress, taking her up to safety and supporting
her as she choked the stinging water from her
lungs. It was Robert who held her, of course, and
her skin tingled where it touched his, his arm
around her waist, holding her back against him.

'Are you all right?' he demanded huskily, as
she panted for breath, and she nodded helplessly,
too distrait to sustain her indignation against him.

'I'm sorry,' she mumbled. She always seemed
to be saying that to him. 'That was a stupid
thing to do.'

'I don't suppose you did it on purpose, did
you?' he taunted her a little mockingly, as he
kicked out strongly for the side, and she was too
weak to make any protest.

He pushed her up on to the side when they got
there, and then dragged himself out beside her,

taking gulping draughts of breath into his own lungs. It was only then she realised what a strain it must have been for him, and she put out her hand to thank him, her fingers touching the smooth skin of his shoulder.

'You must think I'm an awful nuisance,' she murmured, and he turned his head to look at her, his eyes cool and dispassionate.

'I think you should go and take off those wet pants,' he declared flatly, and she withdrew her fingers as if he had burned them.

'I—I—yes, of course,' she stammered, getting to her feet, and this time she didn't make any mistake in her choice of direction.

By the time she came downstairs again Mark and his mother were eating breakfast on the patio, and he called to her as she crossed the hall.

'Come and join us,' he invited, getting to his feet, and she automatically gravitated towards them. 'I thought you were never going to get up,' Mark continued, after they had exchanged greetings. 'I've already been in the pool, and I can tell you, it's fantastic!'

'Tobie's hair's wet,' his mother pointed out, as the girl allowed Mark to help her into her seat. 'Have you been swimming too, my dear, or am I mistaken?'

Tobie smoothed her moist palms down over the sides of her purple denim skirt. With the soaking baggy pants hanging in her bathroom, she was loath to tell a lie, but she had given Robert her word.

'A shower, Mrs Newman,' she answered,

allowing Mark to squeeze her hand under cover of the tabletop. 'I hope you don't mind my coming to the table with wet hair, but I didn't have a drier.'

'There's a hand-drier in the downstairs bathroom,' Mark's mother declared tightly, her nostrils flaring a little. 'You may use that whenever you like.'

'But not now,' put in Mark firmly, keeping hold of her hand. 'You look delicious, honey. And did you know—you're already acquiring a tan!'

'I know.' With Mark, Tobie could relax. 'So are you.'

'Oh, I just go red,' muttered Mark self-deprecatingly. 'I don't have the kind of skin that tans easily.'

'You're too fair, Mark,' said his mother, helping herself to a warm roll, kept hot beneath a perspex cover. 'Your skin's too sensitive. It's coarser skins that tan.'

'Like mine, you mean, Mrs Newman,' observed Tobie shortly, stung by the implied criticism, but the older woman was not perturbed.

'That's right,' she essayed politely, spreading her roll with butter. 'I'm sure you must agree.'

'There could be a kinder way of saying it, Mother,' Mark interposed, shrugging his shoulders helplessly in Tobie's direction. 'I wish I did go brown. Brown skin is so much—nicer.'

'But not necessarily healthier,' insisted his mother firmly. 'Why don't you ring for Monique, Mark, I'm sure Tobie must be hungry.'

In fact, Tobie was not, but she didn't argue.

While Mark went to summon the West Indian maid, she endeavoured to control the indignation his mother deliberately provoked, and wondered again whether there was not more to Mrs Newman's antagonism than she yet understood.

Fan-backed wicker chairs had been set at the circular glass table, and with the breeze rippling the glassy waters of the pool and the whole panorama of the harbour spread out below them, it was an ideal situation. A blue and gold striped awning had been let out from the terrace, giving protection from the strengthening rays of the sun, and later in the day, the shadow of the house itself would provide an oasis of shade.

'What are your plans for the day, Mark?' his mother asked, after Tobie had been provided with orange juice and coffee, and a generous slice of fresh melon. 'I told Cilla you'd be here, and she said she'd come over this morning. Robert won't be here. Lately, he spends most of his mornings working, and I hoped you might invite her to join you for a swim.'

Mark's face mirrored his impatience. 'Damn,' he said, wiping his mouth on his napkin before thrusting it aside. 'Mother, you know Tobie and I only have two weeks! Surely you could have asked me before unloading Cilla on to us.'

Mrs Newman's somewhat heavy features stiffened. 'I am not *unloading* Cilla on to you, Mark. She's a lovely girl. And I don't think it's unreasonable that I should ask you to spend some time with her. Heavens, she has so little company! Without Robert—'

'No one asked the Jennings to stay on the island,' Mark retorted, without compassion. 'If Harvey moved to Martinique or Trinidad—or even the States, for that matter, he could do a useful job of work, and Cilla could mix with people of her own age all the time.'

His mother stared at him with real dislike now. 'Well, that's your opinion, Mark,' she declared, and the glance she cast in Tobie's direction included her in her general disagreement. 'As usual, it's too much trouble for you to be kind to Cilla, even though you know I genuinely care about her. I assume you've forgotten everything I've done for you in the past.'

'Oh, Mother!'

Mark sounded reluctant now, and Tobie wished they could have conducted this argument without her involvement. It was obviously of long standing, and she wondered if Mark had got his mother's feelings confused. Perhaps it was Mark and not Robert she expected Cilla to marry, which put an entirely different light on her hostility.

'Oh, don't mind me,' Mrs Newman was saying now. 'I know my feelings count for little where you're concerned.'

'That's not true, Mother—'

'It is true. You don't care about me. You're only interested in yourself, in your feelings, in the things you want to do!'

'Mother, please. . .'

Mark tried to placate her, but Mrs Newman was determined to have her pound of flesh.

'It doesn't matter that I've sacrificed myself so

that you could go to college, get your degree, take your medical training—'

'Mother!' Mark eventually silenced her with a conciliatory embrace, squeezing her ample body close to him and soothing her with a gentle caress. 'All right, all right. Cilla can come with us, can't she, Tobie?'

Tobie turned her face away from this awful exhibition of moral subjugation and moved her shoulders in a dismissing shrug. What could she say? Certainly nothing that would make him change his mind.

'I was going to suggest taking Tobie to Lobster Cove,' Mark went on humiliatingly, apparently unaware of her lack of enthusiasm. 'I sorted out the snorkelling gear, and I thought we might take a look at the reef.'

Mrs Newman pulled out her handkerchief and sniffed into it before replying. But when she did speak, she was all fluttering concern. 'Well, do take care, won't you, darling?' she exclaimed, all her animosity dispersing now that she had got her own way. 'The reef can be dangerous, and I don't know what I'd do if anything happened to you.'

'Don't be silly.' Mark patted her arm, before releasing her. 'I'll be careful, and Cilla's quite an expert in underwater swimming, isn't she?'

'Experienced,' agreed his mother, nodding. 'Oh, I know she'll be pleased. She's been so much looking forward to your visit.'

Mark seemed to realise that this kind of conversation was hardly flattering to Tobie, and he got to his feet somewhat awkwardly, and made a display of stretching his arms. Then he came behind her chair, running smoothing fingers down her arms from shoulder to elbow, silently assuring her of his real intent. His actions did not please his mother, that much was obvious, but evidently Mrs Newman decided she had shown her hand sufficiently for one morning. With a tight smile she rose too, and making some excuse about speaking to Monique, she left them alone.

Immediately, Mark compelled Tobie up into his arms, finding her lips with his and kissing her deeply. 'Sorry about that, honey,' he said, against her ear. 'But you see how it is. What could I do?'

Tobie could have told him, but it wouldn't do to start an argument, the first real day of their holiday. Besides, Cilla was probably a very nice girl, she told herself firmly, and her presence would preclude any intimacy on Mark's behalf. She was still not ready to commit herself in that way, and she could quite see that here on the island it was going to become increasingly difficult to keep him at arm's length.

Cilla arrived about fifteen minutes later, driving a battered old Mini that had obviously seen better days. She came running up the steps from the courtyard, small and slender, in cotton shorts and a halter top, her cap of dark hair gleaming softly in the sunlight. Tobie guessed she was about twenty-two or twenty-three, her own age, but her lack of make-up and the immaturity of her figure made her appear younger.

'Mark!' she cried, when she saw him stretched

out with Tobie on an airbed beside the pool. 'Oh, Mark, it's good to see you!'

Mark vaulted politely to his feet, his handsome face creasing into a formal smile. 'Cilla!' he greeted her stiffly. 'It's good to see you, too. How are you?'

'I'm fine.' Cilla lifted her shoulders in a little gesture of pleasure as she halted in front of him. 'You look well. Your mother worries about you, but you seem to be thriving.'

'Oh, I am.' Mark visibly relaxed beneath her casual friendliness. 'You know what she's like, always worrying about something or other.'

'Yes.'

Cilla's laugh was conspiratorial, and when her eyes moved to Tobie, Mark remembered his manners.

'Honey,' he said, as Tobie crossed her legs and sat up, 'I guess I don't have to introduce you, but I will anyway. This is Cilla Jennings, our only neighbour. Cilla, meet Tobie Kennedy, my fiancée.'

Tobie's eyes glinted impatiently at him for his deliberate distortion of the truth, but she smiled without rancour at Cilla, liking her more than she had truthfully expected.

'Won't you sit down?' she suggested, indicating the lounger beside her. 'It's too hot to stand on ceremony.'

'Thanks.' Cilla perched on the edge of the chair, grinning at both of them, obviously not at all perturbed by what she had just heard. 'So— how are you enjoying your holiday so far?'

'Very much.' Tobie resisted Mark's efforts to draw her back against him as he came down beside her again. 'I've never been to the Caribbean before.'

'Haven't you?' Cilla sounded almost amazed. Then, taking a deep breath, she turned to survey her surroundings. 'Well, I think this is the most beautiful place on earth.'

'I suppose you know the islands very well,' Tobie said politely, and Cilla turned back to look at her.

'Reasonably,' she admitted. 'Daddy's taken me to Jamaica and Martinique, and Robert and I have sailed to lots of the smaller islands.'

Robert and I? Tobie's tongue clove to the roof of her mouth. She had said it so *casually*.

'Cilla sometimes crews for Rob,' Mark commented, as if Tobie's sudden silence required some explanation. 'She's quite an expert sailor, aren't you, Cilla?'

Cilla was apparently an expert at many things, thought Tobie, trying not to feel bitchy. But that remark about Robert had really thrown her. Somehow, since learning of his incapacitation, she had dismissed her notions of his involvement with other women. But suddenly she was realising how naïve she had been. Robert was still Robert, in spite of his debility, and her own reactions that morning should have alerted her to the awareness that he still possessed the magnetic attraction that women seemed to find irresistible.

'Do you like sailing, Tobie?' Cilla asked now,

and with a wrench Tobie dragged her thoughts back to the present.

'What—oh! Oh, I don't know.' She shook her head regretfully. 'I'm afraid I'm a novice when it comes to boats.'

'Like me,' approved Mark, earning her gratitude for his support. 'Anyway, you aren't thinking of going sailing this morning, are you, Cilla? I thought you might like to come with us to Lobster Cove. I'm going to teach Tobie how to snorkel.'

'Oh, that would be nice,' exclaimed Cilla apologetically, 'but I'm afraid I can't. I promised Robert I'd come over and help him clear those old canvases out of the storeroom.'

Mark, contrarily, looked put out now. 'Hey, come on,' he exclaimed. 'You can help Rob clear out the storeroom any time—'

'I can't.' Cilla got determinedly to her feet. 'We've had to wait until he finished that portrait of Mrs Booth Harrington, and if he starts work again—'

'One day! One morning!' demanded Mark disparagingly, but she was adamant.

'I'm sure you and your fiancée will be much happier without me tagging along,' she declared, winking at Tobie, who returned her stare solemnly. 'Where is Robert, by the way? Do you know?'

'We haven't seen him this morning,' retorted Mark grumpily, and then, realising he was arguing against something which earlier he had objected to, he changed his tone. 'I expect he's in his studio. But I shouldn't disturb him, if I were you. He doesn't take well to intrusions.'

'Oh, I'm not an intruder,' asserted Cilla confidently. 'I'll see you two later, then.' She set off in the direction Robert had pointed out to Tobie the previous day. 'Enjoy yourselves!'

With her departure, Mark made another attempt to put his arms around Tobie, but again she repulsed him, getting to her feet and pacing restlessly across the patio.

'Why did you tell Cilla that I was your fiancée?' she demanded, turning to face him impatiently. 'Our marriage has never been discussed, and I don't care to be told something like that when I can't retaliate.'

Mark sighed, resting back on his elbows. He was wearing shorts, and his white legs stuck out conspicuously from their pale blue cuffs. Already a few freckles had appeared across his nose, but Tobie found herself comparing him unfavourably with Robert's dark-skinned complexion. It didn't help to know that half her anger with Mark was motivated by the proprietorial air Cilla had adopted towards his half-brother, and frustration churned like turbulence inside her.

'It's only a matter of time before we get engaged,' he protested soothingly. 'You know that and I know that, so what are you getting so steamed up about?'

Tobie didn't honestly know. Expelling her breath swiftly, she said the first thing that came into her head. 'You didn't tell your mother that, when she was lining you up with Cilla, did you?'

she exclaimed. 'Oh, no, then it was much easier to let her think we were just holidaying together!'

Mark gazed up at her for a startled moment, then he sprang delightedly to his feet. 'You're jealous!' he cried, grasping her by her shoulders. 'Tobie, you're *jealous*! Hell, don't you know you have no reason to be? I love you, only you. I only agreed to take Cilla to keep my mother happy.'

Tobie tore herself away from him, angry with herself now for precipitating such a scene. 'I am not jealous,' she contradicted him shortly. 'Heavens, I don't care if you fetch half a dozen girls along with us! Just so long as you don't go giving people the wrong ideas about our relationship!'

Mark's face dropped. 'Tobie!' he exclaimed woundedly. 'What did I do? What did I say? I only wanted to show Cilla how things stood between us.'

'No.' Tobie could not let him get away with that. 'You were using me, Mark, as protection. You thought, if Cilla got the picture, she wouldn't cause any problems you couldn't handle.'

'What do you mean?'

'I mean your mother, that's who I mean!' retorted Tobie coldly, and then wrapped her arms about herself protectively as she realised they were rowing in earnest now.

Mark shook his head. 'I don't understand you.'

'Don't you?' Tobie's anger dispersed as quickly as it had appeared. 'No, perhaps you don't. Perhaps that's how I know we're not ready for that kind of commitment yet.'

Mark took a step towards her. 'Look, whatever I said, don't be like this. Don't speak to me like this.' He spread his hands. 'Okay, maybe I did give in too easily this morning, but Mother has done a lot for—'

'Oh, please.' Tobie didn't want to hear this. 'Mark, forget it! I've said my say now, so let's leave it, shall we?'

'You mean you've forgiven me?'

'What's to forgive?' Tobie shook her head. 'Look, are we going to Lobster Cove or aren't we? It's after ten.'

Mark touched her arm. 'Friends?' he asked tentatively, and compassion vied with the exasperation he aroused in her.

'Friends,' she muttered, turning abruptly away. 'I'll get my sunglasses. Wait for me.'

CHAPTER FOUR

IN the event, Tobie enjoyed the trip to Lobster Cove.

Whether it was that each of them in their own way was trying particularly hard to please the other, she couldn't be sure, but one thing was certain, Mark gave her no further cause to feel any resentment towards him. On the contrary, he was a cheerful companion and a patient instructor, and their forays out to the reef proved so captivating, Tobie forgot everything but her gratitude that he should have shown her this new and exciting world.

Until now she had swum underwater only rarely, and then relying on the strength of her lungs to support her. Learning to swim with a snorkel was different, and she could remain submerged for much longer periods.

The most exciting thing of all was the enormous variety of fish and plant life to be found in the pools and crevasses around the reef. She was amazed at how little notice the fish took of her, and the exotic colours of their scales and their weird expressions were a continuous fascination. It seemed hardly credible that the coral itself was a living thing, growing and expanding, in spite of the ceaseless battering of the surf, its mysterious shapes and crenellations forming and reforming over hundreds of years.

It was early afternoon by the time they arrived back at the villa, and it was obvious from the table in the dining room that the rest of the household had already eaten. However, the meal had been a cold buffet, and Mark immediately began helping himself to wedges of quiche, and stuffed olives, indicating with his eyebrows that Tobie should do the same.

'I'm starving, aren't you?' he demanded, when he emptied his mouth sufficiently to speak. 'Hmm,' he picked up a half empty bottle of red wine and sniffed it, 'the '57, no less. Cilla must have stayed for lunch.'

'Actually, I'd prefer to go and take a shower,' Tobie said quietly, her own exhilaration at the morning's expedition fading as the influence of remembered emotions once more cast their web about her. 'I feel hot and sticky, and I'd like to wash the salt out of my hair.'

Mark shrugged. 'Couldn't you do that later?'

Tobie sighed. 'I'm a little tired, too. Perhaps I'll just miss lunch and have a rest.'

'All right.' Mark frowned, but he didn't argue. 'I'll see you soon, then.'

Tobie nodded, and left the room with some relief, mounting the stairs on legs that refused to dawdle. She was eager to escape before Mrs Newman appeared and demanded an explanation for their tardiness, and she breathed in relief when she closed the door of her room behind her.

Once there, however, the reasons for her panic

seemed ridiculous. She wasn't afraid of Mark's mother. On the contrary, she thought she understood her very well. What she wanted to avoid, she realised, was the kind of discussion about Robert that aroused emotions she neither recognised nor wanted to.

After taking a cool shower, she felt more capable of handling the situation. She was allowing what had happened in the past to colour the present, she told herself reasonably, and it was foolish. Robert didn't remember her. They were strangers. And she could hardly blame him for creating these circumstances, when she had known what to expect before she came here.

But had she? Seated before the vanity unit, running her brush through the damp coils of her hair, she realised she had not anticipated anything like this. For one thing, she had expected Robert to recognise her, and for another she had known nothing about his injuries. The bitterness she had felt over losing the only thing she had left to care about languished beside the truth, now that it was revealed to her, and the knowledge that Robert had known nothing of her frantic efforts to see him cast an entirely different light on what came after.

Yet nothing could alter the fact that they had quarrelled, and violently, or change the cruel things that he had said. He had not wanted her then, and he certainly did not want her now, so why was she allowing his presence to create so many problems in her life? Let Cilla run after him; let her fetch and carry for him; let her find out what manner of man he really was.

Going downstairs again some time later, Tobie felt more relaxed than she had done since coming to Emerald Cay. Bringing out her fears and facing them, she had realised how pathetic they really were, and her step was lighter as she came down into the hall.

With the skirt of her cheesecloth dress swinging about her slim legs, she crossed the polished floor in search of Mark. She had worn the dress deliberately. It was one of his favourites, and she knew its lilac colour suited her honey-gold complexion. Besides, it was a little more formal than the skirts and pants she had worn so far, and she needed the fillip it gave her.

The hall, garden room, and pool area were deserted, however, and she was turning back with a puzzled frown puckering her brow when Mark's mother came out of the house behind her.

'If you're looking for Mark, he's not here,' she declared without preamble. 'He and Cilla have gone to play tennis, and I don't expect he'll be back much before dinner.'

'I see.' Tobie glanced surreptitiously at the slim gold watch on her wrist. It was barely four. 'Where are they playing?'

'At the Jennings' house,' replied Mrs Newman with evident satisfaction. 'Shall I ask Monique to bring you some tea? I was just about to go and lie down for an hour.'

'Oh, I—no, that's all right.' Tobie shook her head. 'You go ahead. I'll sunbathe for a while.'

'Very well.'

Mrs Newman disappeared again as swiftly as she had come, and Tobie felt her new-found euphoria disappearing just as quickly. It obviously hadn't taken his mother long to persuade Mark where his duty lay, and while Tobie had no objections to his playing tennis with Cilla, she couldn't help wishing he had told her what he planned to do.

Then she sighed. She was being unreasonable. She had told Mark she was going to rest, and he had probably hesitated to disturb her. How would she have felt if she had been fast asleep and he had come knocking at her door, just to tell her he was going to play tennis with someone else?

She straightened her spine and sauntered determinedly across to the pool. That was what had happened, she decided firmly. Mark had only been thinking of her. So why did she have this irritating feeling that once again he had taken the easy way out?

Pressing her lips together, she swung round on her heels and surveyed the poolside area. It was like a scene from a movie, she thought cynically. Cushioned loungers, a swing couch, changing *cabañas*, and the glinting green waters of the pool itself. But how quickly her isolation began to pall!

Taking a deep breath, she walked to the top of the steps overlooking the courtyard below. Vines and bougainvillaea grew along the wall that separated the two levels, and there was a small waterfall tumbling into a rocky basin, that provided the cooling sound of running water.

Tilting her head, she looked up at the arc of

sky above her. No clouds marred the translucence of the atmosphere, and the brilliance of the light made her eyes ache. Nothing living moved, and without the yacht lying in the harbour below her she could almost believe she was alone on the island.

Dropping her head again, she turned back towards the house, intending to go indoors and get the paperback novel she had brought with her. But halfway across the patio she halted once more, her eyes irresistibly drawn to the path that ran round the side of the house. It was the way to Robert's studio. He had told her yesterday, and Cilla had gone that way this morning.

On impulse she strolled towards the path, glancing at the house as she did so, as if to assure herself that she was not being observed. It sloped slightly downwards as it circled the jutting wing of the main building and then disappeared from view beyond a clump of rose bushes. A tantalising challenge, and one she was powerless to resist.

Why not? she asked herself impatiently, as she started along the path, which was wide enough to take Robert's wheelchair. She needn't go right along it. As soon as she saw Robert's studio she would turn back, and if he saw her, what could he say? She could always pretend she had come along in all innocence, and he was unlikely to call her a liar.

She caught her dress on the rose bushes, and scratched her arm freeing herself, which didn't please her. She thought, rather resentfully, that Robert might have had the decency to keep the way clear, and then grimaced at her own audacity. After all, he hadn't invited her to come along here, and no doubt Cilla managed without accident. But then Cilla was small and slim and unlikely to wear something so unsuitable to come calling.

The path eventually opened out before a single-storied extension that was almost completely made of glass. Long, sloping panels had been let into the roof, and the walls from floor to ceiling were sheets of plate glass. It was completely private. There was no access, other than by the way she had come, and below the wide courtyard the ground fell away steeply to the rocks beneath.

Tobie hesitated. The place seemed deserted, and for the first time she wondered if Robert had gone with his half-brother and Cilla. It was possible—no, it was probable. After all, Cilla must have been with Robert when they got back after lunch, and Mrs Newman was unlikely to have been so tactless as to suggest that Cilla abandoned Robert to play tennis with the fitter man.

With a sigh of frustration Tobie crossed the flat stones to stare dispiritedly through the windows of the studio. It was like the studio Robert had had in London. Lots of canvases, finished and unfinished, were stacked against the walls. There were tubes of paint, tins of varnish, jars containing dozens of brushes and knives. An easel was propped in the middle of the floor, with a sheet draped over it, which seemed to indicate, as Cilla had said, that he wasn't working on anything at the moment, and the stool he apparently used to sit on was standing forlornly before it. It reminded her poignantly of how close they had once been, of the times she had insisted on tidying up his studio, and of his mocking response to her spurts of housewifely zeal. They had usually ended in his making love to her, and her desire for industry had been replaced by her eager desire for him, and the demanding hunger of his possession. . .

The sound of someone coming aroused Tobie to an uneasy awareness of her surroundings. She guessed it must be Mrs Newman, who had observed her trespass, and she looked about her desperately, searching for somewhere to hide. She could imagine the other woman's scathing comments if she found her peering in her son's studio, and it would be doubly embarrassing if she confided as much to Robert himself.

But there was nowhere to hide, and she was standing there feeling ridiculously chastened, when a tall, jeanclad figure came around the corner. It was not Mrs Newman, it was Robert himself, propelling himself firmly with two sticks, and her face flamed at the thought of what he must be thinking.

He halted abruptly when he saw her by the studio windows, and she wished, ridiculously, that she was one of those helpless feminine women who could get away with anything by assuming innocence. If she could have pretended she had lost her way, or feigned ignorance of her whereabouts, she might have got away with it, even if they both knew that she was lying. But she wasn't able to do that. Dissembling did not come easy to her, and she simply wasn't the type to plead weakness.

So she straightened determinedly, and adopting a confident smile, said: 'Hello there! I hope you don't mind, but I was curious to see where you worked.'

Robert remained stationary for a few seconds longer, and then with an indifferent shrug he came towards her. Tobie suspected he would prefer her to avert her gaze from the inco-ordination of his movements, but she couldn't drag her eyes away, and his mouth hardened as he covered the space between them. However, he didn't stop to speak to her. He went past her, propping his sticks against the wall as he unlocked the studio, sliding the door aside before turning his head to look at her.

'You'd better come in, hadn't you?' he suggested, his voice without expression, and with some misgivings she complied.

The smell was achingly familiar, that mingling of oils and resin, paint and canvas, that reminded her of the skill and effort he had always put into his work. She had always found it exciting that the hands which had held her and caressed her and aroused such wanton emotions inside her could create such inspirational masterpieces of art. Those long narrow-boned fingers possessed intelligence and sensitivity, and he had used both when he was making love to her.

'I—I thought perhaps you'd gone with Mark and Cilla,' Tobie ventured now, as Robert supported himself against a paint-smeared table, and his mouth took on a sardonic twist.

'Unfortunately, as you can see, I'm not much good on a tennis court,' he returned dryly, and Tobie felt her colour deepening.

'I—I didn't mean—'

'I know.' There was impatience in the response. 'However, I find no pleasure in watching two people chase a ball around a court, and besides, like you, I preferred my own company.'

Tobie lifted her head. 'Is that meant to be insulting?'

'No.' He shrugged his lean shoulders. 'Just a statement of fact.'

'You didn't feel that way this morning,' Tobie countered, allowing her fingers to pluck at the corner of a rolled canvas, and he gave her a searching look.

'I wasn't aware my activities were the focus of so much scrutiny,' he commented pointedly. 'However, if you're referring to Cilla Jennings, you're right. She's an undemanding little soul, and she has this desperate need to make herself indispensable to everyone.'

Not to everyone, thought Tobie tightly, but she couldn't say so.

'She seems a nice girl,' she said instead, moving away from the door to examine a half-finished canvas, propped carelessly against the far wall. 'This is good. Aren't you going to finish it?'

'It's a mess,' retorted Robert dispassionately. 'I thought you said you knew about painting. The colouring has no depth, and the texture of the subject's skin is all wrong.'

'I didn't say I knew about painting,' Tobie contradicted hotly. 'You said—'

'Well, never mind.' Robert pushed back an errant strand of his thick dark hair with an impatient hand. 'And so far as Cilla is concerned, she is a nice girl. She has a lonely life at home, with only her father for company. She seems to enjoy coming here. No doubt even the companionship of a middle-aged paraplegic is better than nothing.'

'You're neither middle-aged nor a paraplegic!' exclaimed Tobie, without thinking, scrambling to her feet to face him angrily. 'And you don't believe that any more than I do!'

'No?' Robert's heavy-lidded eyes held hers fast. 'And what would you know about it?'

Tobie endeavoured to repair the damage done by her impetuous tongue. 'What I meant to say was—'

'I think you've said quite enough,' he interrupted her curtly. 'Perhaps I ought to ask why you're not keeping your fiancé company, instead of wasting my time!'

Tobie's face burned. 'Is that what you think?' she exclaimed, shaken by his unexpected cruelty. 'That—that I'm wasting your time?' Her lips trembled and she struggled to control them. Almost blindly she turned towards the door. 'Well, never let it be said that I—'

'Wait! Tobie, wait!' His exasperated use of her name arrested her, and he repeated it again as he dragged himself across the floor to where she was standing. 'I'm sorry, I shouldn't have said that. It wasn't true. You're not wasting my time. I didn't plan to work this afternoon anyway.'

'Didn't you?' She turned to find him right behind her, and his nearness was an assault on her already disturbed senses. He was supporting himself without his sticks, and in spite of her heels he was still a couple of inches taller than she was, lean and dark and disruptively attractive, the opened neck of his shirt emitting an odour of warmth and cleanliness, and unmistakable maleness.

'No, I didn't,' he agreed brusquely. 'I was just being thoroughly objectionable. I'm sorry, I didn't intend to hurt your feelings.'

Her feelings! Dear God, did he have any idea what he was doing to her feelings standing near her like this? she wondered faintly. His body was a mere handsbreadth from hers, and her hands itched to reach out and make contact. She had actually to clench them at her sides to prevent herself from doing so, and her breathing felt constricted as she fought frantically to remain calm. But it wasn't easy when she was this close to him, and all the remembered intimacy they had shared enveloped her in its tenuous threads.

'Look, let me make amends,' he offered quietly. 'Let me show you a little of my island, hmm? I doubt Mark's had the time yet to take you to Lotus Point, has he?'

Tobie's hands sought the sliding door behind her, pressing it aside so that she could step backward into the courtyard. 'I really think I ought to go back to the house,' she murmured uncomfortably. 'M-Mark will be home soon. He may wonder where I am.'

'Mark won't be home before dark,' retorted Robert flatly, reaching for his sticks. 'I know the Jennings, and Harvey won't let him go without offering some refreshment.'

'Your—your mother said he'd be back before dinner,' Tobie insisted.

'Doubtless he will. But as dinner isn't until eight o'clock, you'll agree he has plenty of time.'

Tobie bent her head. 'You really want me to come with you?'

Robert hesitated. 'I invited you, didn't I?'

'Yes—'

'If what you're trying to say is that you'd rather not go, come right out and say it,' he remarked dryly. 'I won't be offended. I promise.'

Tobie's head jerked up. 'You have no reason for thinking that,' she protested, and he stepped out on to the square stones of the courtyard.

'Haven't I?' His tone had hardened slightly, but as if he was determined not to have any further argument with her, he became persuasive once more. 'Very well, then. The least I can do is entertain Mark's girl-friend in his absence. Do you want to come or don't you?'

Tobie drew an unsteady breath. 'Does—does Henri drive you?'

'No.' Now Robert's face darkened with colour. 'I drive myself,' he retorted tersely. 'I'm normally quite reliable. The jeep is fitted with hand controls, and I usually manage to curb my desire for speed. Does that reassure you? Or does my present condition disprove that theory?'

Tobie moved her shoulders helplessly. 'All right, I'll come.'

'Thank you.'

Robert's lips twisted in self-mockery as she turned away, and she had the instinctive belief that she should not have given in to him.

She was half afraid she might meet his mother as she ran back to the house for her sunglasses. The last thing she wanted right now was that woman's piercing regard penetrating her crumbling defences, exposing the sudden vulnerability of her emotions. She had never expected to find herself in a situation where she might actually feel sorry for Robert, and perhaps she owed him something for the good times they had shared. If they could be friends, and not enemies, she might conceivably find with Mark the happiness she knew he wanted to give her.

Happily, Mrs Newman's rooms were in a different wing of the house, and no one but Monique was about when she came downstairs again. The black maid gave her her white-toothed grin, and then asked whether she would like tea.

'Not right now, Monique, thank you,' Tobie refused politely. 'I'm going out with Mr Lang. Would you tell Mr Newman where I am if he comes back?'

'Sure thing, Miss Kennedy.' Monique's Americanisms were indicative of the amount of television she watched. 'Have a good day!'

'Thank you.'

Tobie smiled, and hastened across the patio, and the fact that she hadn't eaten or drunk anything since breakfast didn't occur to her.

The beach buggy that she and Mark had used the previous afternoon was parked at the foot of the steps with Robert behind the wheel. She guessed he found an immense difference in driving this small utility to the expensive sports cars he had once favoured, but he handled both with the same skill. Except on that one occasion, she thought regretfully, as he drove smoothly out on to the road.

The air was cooler as the heat of the day subsided, and it was deliciously refreshing, feeling the breeze tugging at her hair. They might have been any young couple out for a drive, she mused, as she speculated on the premise of how deceptive appearances could be. And instead of two ordinary people, enjoying an afternoon outing, they were protagonists in a lurid melodrama, with all the characters playing different roles, each of them knowing their own lines, but no one else's. It was a kind of method play, governed by audience participation, with the outcome always in doubt.

'You're very quiet.'

Robert's remark was accompanied by a swift sideways glance, and Tobie endeavoured to shed the disturbing melancholia that had gripped her.

'I was just thinking,' she murmured, pushing her dark glasses further up her nose. 'Isn't that the way to the cove Mark took me to this morning?'

'That's right.' Robert barely glanced at the track, that wound around the thickly-wooded hillside and down to the tiny bay, before returning to his theme. 'What were you thinking about? You seemed very solemn.'

'Oh. . .' Tobie put up a nervous hand to her hair, 'nothing in particular. I guess I was just dreaming. It's so beautiful here. I envy you.'

'Do you?' Robert's tone was sardonic. 'I doubt you do.' He ran a knowing hand over his thigh. 'I can't believe you'd want to give up your freedom for this.'

She sighed. 'I meant I envied you the island, you know that. Besides,' she licked her dry lips, 'you're obviously improving. You'll probably be walking without sticks before long—'

'*No*!' His denial was harsh and abrupt. 'No, that's not possible.' He shook his head. 'Oh, sure, I've learned to stand on my own two feet again, and no one has to carry me around like a baby any more. But there's only so much one can do, so far one can go. And I guess I've reached my limit.'

'So why don't you want your mother and Mark to know?' asked Tobie, before she could prevent herself. 'I mean, they care about you, don't they? Don't you think they have a right to know?'

Robert's long fingers curved around the wheel. 'That's my affair,' he replied tautly, and she realised she had overstepped herself once more.

The wildness of the interior of the island gave way once again to sun-bleached rocks and coral sands, and Robert drove down a twisting track to

a promontory of land that projected into the sea,
like a horny finger pointing towards the reef.
'Lotus Point,' he observed, without expression,
and brought the buggy to a standstill above a
shelving, ragged coastline.

Tobie glanced at his set face, and then, feeling
restless, she climbed out of the vehicle. The
breeze was much stronger here, bending the
twisted boles of a sprawling cypress, magnifying
the cries of the gulls and the constant thunder of
the surf on the reef. It was a lonely place, less
civilised in appearance than those parts of the
island she had seen so far, and yet as beautiful
in its way as the calmer waters of the lagoon.

Robert had pulled out a pack of narrow cigars,
and she heard the flick of his lighter as he applied
the flame. She was reluctant to intrude upon his
chosen isolation, and leaving the buggy, she
walked to the edge of the cliff and looked down.

It was not as steep as she had expected. Shallow
outcroppings of rock provided natural footholds,
and she realised it was possible to climb down
to sea level. There were pools among the rocks,
some of them quite deep, and constantly filled
and refilled by the surging tide. They were the
habitat of crab and lobster, and other shellfish that
clung to the sea-smoothed crags, and the receding
swell exposed their weed-strewn depths.

But the constant movement of the water began
to have a different effect upon her. A curious
giddiness assailed her, and she stumbled back
from the edge, dropping down on to her knees as
the earth and sky swam unsteadily about her.

'Tobie!'

Robert's call came from the beach buggy, but she felt too dizzy to make her way back to him. Perhaps if she just remained completely still for a few moments, the feeling would go away. The last thing she wanted to have to do was to make a nuisance of herself now.

'*Tobie*!'

This time the voice was much nearer, and she managed to hold up her head sufficiently to see that he was coming towards her on his sticks. He dropped them when he was within a few feet of her, kneeling down beside her and putting cool fingers on her sticky forehead.

'What's wrong?' he demanded, his fingers moving from her temple to her chin, tipping her face up to his. 'Are you ill? Is it the heat?'

His concern was reassuring, but she pulled her chin away from those disturbing fingers, saying tautly: 'That—that's probably what it is. The heat, I mean. I just felt sick, and—and a little dizzy.'

'Dizzy?' His eyes narrowed. 'Are you thirsty? When did you last have anything to drink?'

Tobie moved her head dazedly from side to side. 'I don't know. Yes, yes, I do. It—it was this morning—'

'*This morning*!' His response was violent. 'You mean you haven't had anything to drink since this morning?'

'I—don't think so—'

'You crazy little fool!' He brought his fist down hard on the turf beside him. 'And you went swimming this morning, didn't you?'

'Yes, but—'

'You did have some lunch?'

Tobie sighed. 'Actually, no—'

The word he used was very short and succinct, and also very crude. 'Are you out of your mind?' he demanded. struggling to his feet and hauling her up with him. 'Don't you realise how easily you can get dehydrated in this climate?'

'I didn't think.' Tobie endeavoured to free herself from his grasp, but he was amazingly strong, and with his arm around her back, supporting her, she was tempted to give in and let him take her weight. But with the hardness of his muscular body next to hers, and the smell of his warm skin filling her nostrils, she realised the dangers of simple promiscuity better than he did. At the moment, she was his half-brother's girl-friend, and as such she warranted his consideration. But if, acting under influences she had thought forgotten, she did anything to unbalance the status quo, she and not Robert would be to blame.

'I think there are some cans of beer under the back seat of the jeep,' he was saying now, brushing aside the silky strands of her hair that the wind had blown into his mouth. 'They'll be warm, but I guess they'll serve the purpose.'

'I'm all right, honestly,' Tobie insisted, trying once again to detach herself from him. 'The dizziness has almost gone, and I feel loads better.'

'Good.' He acknowledged her assurance with a faintly mocking smile. 'I'm glad you didn't fall *over* the cliff. Mark would never have forgiven me.' He pulled a wry face. 'Come to think of it, I'd never have forgiven myself.'

'It was my fault,' Tobie said, her lips parting over even white teeth, and his dark eyes grew teasing.

'I'd have had some difficulty convincing Mark of that,' he commented humorously. 'But fortunately I won't have to. You're still in one piece.'

Tobie's smile grew a little fixed as he continued to look at her. He was so close she could feel his breath on her cheek, and feel the bone of his hip digging into hers. Under his scrutiny, her breasts rose and fell in quickened awareness, and when his eyes dropped to the shadowy hollow exposed by the low neckline of her dress, she felt the deepening of his regard.

Then he said something so intensely alarming and shocking that she could hardly control her gulp of dismay, and she was sure he must have detected her sudden instinctive withdrawal.

'Do I know you?' he demanded, gazing into her face. 'Have I seen you before?' He shook his head uncomprehendingly. 'I don't know what it is, but I keep getting this feeling of *déjà vu*.'

CHAPTER FIVE

TOBIE stood on her balcony, watching the sun sink slowly beneath the belt of cloud on the horizon. Its passing turned the sea from orange to red, and finally to deepest purple, its brilliance still reflected in the water even after it had disappeared from her sight.

It was another beautiful evening, the air as warm and soft as velvet. They had not had so much as a shower of rain since their arrival almost a week ago, and her skin was rapidly turning to honey-gold. Even Mark had acquired an all-over pink blush, but he assured her glumly that it would disappear once they got back to London.

To London. . .

Tobie sighed, allowing her palms to curl round the smooth iron of the balcony rail. London seemed so far away, a world away in fact, and with each passing day she felt more and more remote from the demands of everyday existence. Sometimes she told herself she would be glad when the time came for them to leave, but mostly she acknowledged that she was dreading that day coming, and with it the realisation that she might never see Robert again.

She drew a trembling breath. Robert! How easily she had fallen into the trap of her own making. Coming here, meeting him again; she had thought she could handle it. But she couldn't. With each day it became harder, and the hardest thing of all was his persistent detachment. Not once since that afternoon at Lotus Point had he shown her anything but friendly civility, but his continued impersonality was beginning to tell on her nerves. It was what she had wanted, what she had not dared to hope for, yet it left her restless and dissatisfied.

To begin with, she had been relieved when he had drawn back from probing into her identity. She might easily have made mistakes in the chaotic state into which his questioning might have thrown her. His unexpected reaction to her silence had been like a gift from the gods. He had assumed she would object to his advances, and his awareness of her had made him release her.

'I'm sorry,' he had said stiffly, as he drew away. 'You must forgive me. You have a curious effect on people, but I realise you must find my attentions disagreeable.'

Tobie, struggling to regain her balance, had found it difficult to answer him. 'You—you don't have to apologise, Robert,' she said, forestalling his effort to retrieve his sticks, and handing them to him. 'We—I—I'm grateful for your assistance. And—and we all get those feelings from time to time.'

The drive back to Soledad was accomplished almost in silence. Tobie had found diversion in sipping a can of warm beer, and Robert had driven the fifteen miles or so in controlled concentration.

But they each had their own thoughts, and she
wondered what Robert's were.

Since then, however, her association with him
had been limited. Mark persistently staked his
claim, making it manifestly obvious that the afternoon he had spent with Cilla had been pressed
upon him because Tobie was supposedly resting,
and though Cilla had visited Soledad several
times since, she evidently preferred Robert's
company. She and Mark behaved more like
brother and sister, and Mrs Newman continually
baulked at their apparent determination to avoid
a closer relationship.

So far as Tobie was concerned, the situation
had deteriorated. She constantly found her emotions warring with the dictates of her conscience,
and she could no longer deny the feelings of
resentment she experienced every time she saw
Robert and Cilla together. It wasn't that she was
jealous, she argued with herself in her more
reasonable moments. Rather, it was a feeling that
life had treated her so unfairly. The accident
appeared to have altered Robert's personality.
She would never have believed he could be
patient or understanding, and if he was thinking
of marriage now, why couldn't he have done so
before they quarrelled, and he half killed himself?
Sometimes she wondered if he might not have
had second thoughts had things gone differently.
If he hadn't slammed into his car and driven so
recklessly, if she hadn't subsequently suffered the
physical consequences of his rejection, might
they conceivably still have been together, or was

she fooling herself by imagining he had felt any deeper feelings for her than he had for the countless other girls who had shared his bed?

A film of sweat moistened her spine, and she shivered suddenly. It was strange, but since learning of his accident she had conveniently forgotten his selfishness. All her natural animosity towards him had been neutralised by compassion, and only now did she allow the memories she had hitherto avoided to harden her resolve. He was still the same man. She had to accept that fact. And perhaps the time had come for her to stop feeling so guilty.

Turning back into her bedroom, she switched on the lamps and surveyed the room without pleasure. This wasn't Mark's home, she thought with aversion, it was Robert's. This was Robert's furniture. Robert's house, Robert's *island*; it was Robert's money that bought their food, and Robert's aircraft that would eventually take them back to St Lucia. How could she have been so uncaring? She was accepting the hospitality of a man who had destroyed her life once already, and who had it in his power to destroy it yet again?

Expelling her breath on a heavy sigh, she moved towards the vanity unit. Somehow she had to compose herself and get dressed for dinner. The Jennings were joining them this evening, and Mark had especially asked her to wear something nice.

'I want you to stun old Harvey,' he had declared, his hands on her shoulders, his face alight with enthusiasm. 'He never sees anyone except Cilla, and I want him to know what he's missing.'

Tobie had protested, half embarrassed by his eagerness, but Mark had been adamant, and she had promised to choose something flattering. As a matter of fact, she had already decided what she was going to wear. It was a simple black chiffon gown, with a strapless bodice, bloused above a narrow pleated skirt. It exposed her tan, and its mid-length displayed her legs to advantage. It had hardly any back, and with her hair hanging loose from a central parting, she knew she would not disappoint him.

But now, leaning forward to smooth her finger-tips over her cheekbones, Tobie wondered whether it was quite sensible to continue tempting fate. Robert's momentary recognition had proved that somewhere on the periphery of his subconscious, he knew they had met before at least, and if he should betray this knowledge, whether deliberately or otherwise, how might Mark take it now? He might find her reasons for withholding the fact that she had known his brother in London suspect, and if he ever found out the whole truth. . .

She sighed, sinking down on to the end of her bed. Did it really matter, all this soul-searching? Was it worth it? Didn't she really know that she and Mark were unlikely to make it together? And why tonight in any case? Why was she examining her feelings tonight?

She knew the answer. Just before she came to change, Mark had told her that Robert and Cilla planned to fly to Miami the next morning, to meet Robert's agent, and the connotations were obvious.

Time was passing, and Tobie realised she would have to make an effort to get ready. Reaching for a jar of cream, she began to smooth it into her skin, and the rhythmic massage soothed her troubled emotions. It was pointless letting Robert's behaviour have any effect on her behaviour, she told herself severely, and silenced the wayward voice inside her that mocked her feeble protestations.

By the time she was ready she felt infinitely more confident. A greeny-grey mascara had added mystery to the wide-spaced beauty of her eyes, and the lip-lustre she used had given her mouth a shining sensuality. She looked tall and slim and self-assured, yet with an underlying air of diffidence that was both provocative and feminine. She knew she had never looked better, and as she descended the stairs she acknowledged the unworthy thought that Robert might envy his half-brother's good fortune.

The arrangement was that they should all assemble on the patio for drinks before dinner, but when Tobie emerged from the house she thought at first she was the only arrival. The moon-dappled terrace seemed deserted, and the only sound she could hear was the sucking motion of the water against the marbled lip of the pool.

She came out of the shadows into the subdued lighting cast by the floodlighting beneath the pool's surface, and as she did so, the whisper of

Robert's chair wheels alerted her to his presence.

He must have been seated at the far end of the terrace, but now he propelled himself towards her, the glow of his slim cigar like a firefly in the darkness.

'Tobie,' he greeted her politely, acknowledging her with his usual courtesy. 'You and I appear to be the only ones capable of being punctual.'

Tobie allowed a faint smile to tilt the corners of her mouth. 'I'm five minutes late, actually,' she answered inconsequently. 'Unless my watch is wrong.'

Robert consulted the square gold watch on his wrist. 'No,' he remarked smoothly. 'It's after seven-thirty.' He smiled. 'No matter. Can I offer you a drink instead? Monique seems to have supplied most things here.' He indicated the trolley behind them. 'What will you have?'

Tobie took an impatient breath. His reactions, as usual, left her feeling tense and irritated. It was as if he didn't see her as anything more than another human being, an acceptable one perhaps, but not necessarily female.

'I'd like a Bacardi and Coke,' she replied, in answer to his questioning stare, and he turned to attend to it while she stood silently, gazing broodingly down towards the little harbour. She and Mark had driven down there the previous afternoon, and Mark had rowed her out to the yacht, but as yet Robert had not suggested taking them out in it. It seemed he was too busy organising his own affairs, and Mark was content to spend his time alone with Tobie.

'Mark tells me you're going to Miami tomorrow,' she ventured, after he had handed her a tall frosted glass, chinking with ice, and Robert swung his chair round to face her.

'That's right,' he agreed, raising his glass of Scotch towards her in a silent toast. 'I have to see my agent, Rowan Hartley, and the break will do Cilla good. I imagine Mark also told you I was taking Cilla along.'

'Yes.' Tobie swallowed a mouthful of her drink before continuing. 'She's a lucky girl, isn't she? Earning a trip to Miami. You must—think a lot about her.'

'I do.' Robert studied the liquid in his glass. 'Since I came here almost three years ago she's been a good friend, and I owe her a lot.' He paused. 'In the beginning, I had a physiotherapist living here, working with me, but after he left Cilla started to spend more and more time at Soledad.' He shrugged. 'You have to admit, few girls of her age would give up their time to play nurse to an invalid.'

'You're hardly an invalid,' said Tobie tightly, remembering the last conversation like this they had had, and he pulled a wry face.

'I was,' he remarked quietly. 'You're seeing the results of months—*years*—of patient effort.' He sighed. 'If you'd seen me after the crash you'd have wanted to throw up. I was a mess. I couldn't do anything for myself at all. I don't know how many bones were broken, but I do know it's a miracle that my hands survived unscathed.'

Tobie cradled her drink between her two palms. 'I—I suppose so.'

'There's no suppose about it,' retorted Robert, an edge invading his voice. 'I think if I'd lost the ability to paint, along with everything else, I'd have killed myself!'

'*No!*' Tobie was horrified, her face pale in the moonlight, but he was adamant.

'Yes,' he contradicted her harshly, lying back in his chair, his dark face tilted towards her. 'Oh, yes, I'd have done it. I had nothing else to live for.'

Tobie took an uncertain step and sat down rather heavily on the nearby lounger. 'You—you had—your family—' she tendered, but his mouth mocked her faint reproval.

'My family hadn't been around much up until that time,' he essayed dryly. 'A less benevolent individual might have been forgiven for wondering whether the summoning of one's next-of-kin inspires a totally erroneous assessment of one's chances of survival.'

As he spoke, his mouth curved in an exact replica of the smile he had worn three years ago, when he told her that marriage was not among his more immediate concerns. That had been the start of the row which had severed any relationship between them, and although she believed he was unaware of it, it sent an uneasy chill feathering along her spine. But was that why his mother had engineered their reunion? Because she had believed he was dying? And if so, was she aware that her eldest son was as perceptive of her motives as he had ever been?

'So. . .' Robert drawled now, interrupting her troubled speculations, 'have I shocked you? Or am I wrong, and you weren't silently admonishing my ingratitude?'

'I—I—was wondering whether you weren't perhaps being a little hard on your relations,' she conceded tentatively. 'I'm sure Mark's very fond of you.'

Robert frowned, and then shrugged. 'You're probably right,' he agreed flatly. 'Can I get you another drink?'

'I haven't finished this one yet,' she demurred, and he excused himself to pour another measure of Scotch into his own glass.

'So now you know why I'm so fond of Cilla,' he remarked, when he turned to face her again. 'She's the only one I can talk to. And she has no hidden motives.'

Tobie's lips compressed. It was hard, sitting here listening to him extol Cilla's virtues. She would not have been human if she had not felt some indignation at his evident lack of interest in her concerns, and anger made her reckless.

'Perhaps she has,' she said now, meeting his eyes across the rim of her glass. 'Hidden motives, I mean. Only maybe you're not aware of them.'

Robert's eyes narrowed. 'What's that supposed to imply?'

Tobie moved her slim shoulders in a careless gesture. 'I imagine she may have—plans of her own.'

'To marry me?' asked Robert arrogantly, his

dark eyes vaguely amused. 'So what if she has? I'm flattered.'

It was not the response she had expected. In spite of Mark's insinuations, she had not really believed him when he spoke of the relationship between Robert and Cilla. She had anticipated anger or indignation, not complacence, and Robert's somewhat smug self-satisfaction made her want to hurt him as he was unknowingly hurting her.

'I imagine you would be. Flattered, I mean,' she countered, adding unforgivably: 'As you said, there aren't many girls who would want to get involved with someone who couldn't lead a— normal married life!'

His sudden intake of breath was evidence of the effect her words had had upon him. 'I'm not impotent, you know,' he muttered, his face mirroring his repugnance, and Tobie got abruptly to her feet as Cilla's Mini came into the courtyard below them.

It was as well that the lights spilling out from the house cast pools of shadow. Tobie's burning face might have evoked some curious glances. As it was, she sheltered in the concealing darkness, watching with detachment as Cilla and her father mounted the steps to the patio.

'Hello, you two!' In spite of the darkness of Tobie's dress, Cilla had seen her, and after squeezing Robert's outstretched hand in greeting, the other girl turned to her father.

'This is Mark's fiancée, Daddy,' she said, making the necessary introductions. 'My father's an antiquarian, Tobie. He's filled our house with old books and bric-à-brac, and now he spends his time studying them.'

Remembering what Mark had said about Harvey Jennings being a sponger, Tobie was pleasantly surprised to meet the older man. Her first impressions were of a slightly-stooped individual, in his early sixties, whose somewhat lugubrious expression was relieved by the humorous glint of eyes half concealed behind horn-rimmed spectacles.

'How do you do, Miss Kennedy,' he said, shaking her hand firmly. 'I'm delighted to meet you at last. Having heard your praises sung from every quarter, I was eager to see the original for myself.'

Tobie's blush was quite natural in the circumstances, and the reasons for her heated colouring easily explained. 'You're very kind,' she smiled, not daring to look in Robert's direction. 'I only hope I won't disappoint you.'

'Daddy appreciates beautiful things,' observed Cilla, without any trace of envy. 'You must come and see his collection some time.'

'Yes, do,' invited her father, releasing her hand with reluctance. 'I'd be happy to show it to you.'

'Thank you.'

Tobie managed a tight smile, but she was relieved when Robert offered them a drink and she had a few moments to gather her shredded composure. She had never felt more contemptible in her life, and if the ground had opened up beneath her and swallowed her into its murky depths, she felt it would have been nothing more than she deserved. It was all very well blaming Robert for destroying her innocence. He had, and somehow she had to live with that. What was unforgivable was that she had accused a man without defences of being nothing more than a useless shell.

Hands descending on her bare shoulders alerted her to Mark's arrival, and she turned to him almost desperately. 'Where have you been?' she demanded, clutching his arm. 'I've been waiting for you!'

'If I'd known you'd be this pleased to see me, I'd have come sooner,' Mark observed huskily, bending to bestow a kiss on her temple. 'Hmm, you smell delicious. What is it? Something French?'

'It's *Rive Gauche*, actually,' replied Tobie, aware that they had attracted the attention of the other members of the party. 'Look, Cilla and her father are here.'

Mark's smile became a trifle forced as he shook hands with the older man, though his affection for Cilla was real enough. However, after he had helped himself to a drink he returned to Tobie, slipping his arm possessively about her waist and saying softly:

'I'm sorry I wasn't here when you came down, but I've been talking to Mother. She's not too happy about Rob taking Cilla to Miami.'

Tobie thought rather hysterically that she and Mrs Newman were agreed on something at last, but she couldn't say so.

'Not that there's a lot she can do about it,'

admitted Mark dispassionately. 'Cilla's old enough to know what she's doing, and Rob's not likely to be persuaded to change his mind.'

Tobie drew a steadying breath. 'Your mother likes Cilla. Why should she object?'

Mark quirked an eyebrow. 'Oh, yes, she likes Cilla, because she's biddable. But not as Rob's wife.'

'Why?' Tobie was perplexed, and at least the question diverted her mind from more disturbing thoughts.

'Oh——' Mark bent his head, and now she realised he was half embarrassed by her persistence, 'I don't think she feels Rob is——up to the strain of such an undertaking as marriage.'

Tobie's brow furrowed. 'But he's all right——'

'He's not a whole man, Tobie,' Mark interrupted her in a low voice. He sighed. 'Look, I didn't want to have to tell you this, but——well, Rob would be no use to a woman.'

'No——'

'Yes.' Mark was adamant. 'I should know. I've spoken to his physician.'

Tobie could hardly hide her horror at his announcement. It wasn't true, it *couldn't* be true, she told herself without conviction. But the fact remained, Mark was a doctor, and he was unlikely to be mistaken. It was doubly shocking after the way she had taunted Robert earlier, and her stomach heaved at the realisation that his harsh denial had been merely a pitiful defence.

Mrs Newman's appearance precluded any further discussion of the subject, and Tobie was glad. She didn't want to talk about it, she didn't even want to think about it, and she wished with all her heart that she had never had that conversation.

She didn't remember much of the meal that followed. The food was excellent, as usual—a seafood salad followed by barbecued steaks, and a mouthwatering strawberry gateau, that was one of Monique's specialities. Tobie hoped her lack of appetite would go unnoticed, and came out in a cold sweat once when she looked up to find Robert's brooding gaze upon her. But he didn't say anything to upset her digestion, and she concentrated on her plate after that, avoiding another encounter.

Yet, although she kept her eyes averted, she could still see Robert sitting at the head of the table. No matter how she tried, she could not dislodge his image, and she felt an unbearable weight of depression at the things Mark had confided. It made her own feelings earlier that evening seem paltry by comparison, and her head began to ache with the turmoil of her thoughts.

When dinner was over they assembled in the drawing room. Monique's fifteen-year-old daughter, Thérèse, served coffee, and Mark put some records on the turntable. Tobie was alone, sitting on the end of a tapestry-covered sofa, her eyes irresistibly drawn to the man in the dark green velvet suit, with the froth of a lace jabot below his dark tie, his wheelchair drawn close to Cilla's side. The other girl was talking to him, making him smile, and Tobie looked up, almost angrily, when someone blocked her view.

'Do you mind if I join you?'

It was Harvey Jennings, carrying a bottle of Napoleon brandy in one hand and a glass in the other, and Tobie had no reason to object. 'Please—sit down,' she invited, steadying her coffee cup, and with an ungraceful bow he complied.

'Will you have some?' he suggested, waving the bottle of brandy, but Tobie demurred.

'I like my coffee straight,' she said, forcing a smile, and he nodded as he filled his glass.

She thought he hàd had several samples already from the way his hand shook as he poured the liquid, but it was nothing to do with her if he chose to over-imbibe. Perhaps that was why Cilla felt obliged to stay with him, she mused, and then shunned the connotations of that particular train of thought.

'Tell me,' said Harvey, drawing his greying brows together above the rims of his spectacles, 'are you a model, Miss Kennedy?' He seemed to find difficulty in focussing, but he evidently succeeded before adding: 'I seem to know your face from somewhere. You know how it is. Could I have seen it in a magazine? One of those glossy periodicals Cilla has mailed every month?'

'No!' Tobie's negation was swift and anxious, and accompanied by a somewhat apprehensive appraisal of their surroundings. 'I—my face is not unique, Mr Jennings. You're probably confusing me with someone else.'

'I don't think so.' Harvey shook his head, raising his glass to his lips and watching her through thoughtful eyes. 'No, sir, I know that face, Miss Kennedy. Now how could I have seen it before?'

'How about the photograph I showed you a few days ago?' enquired Mark's welcome voice from right behind them, and Harvey turned to him perplexedly.

'Did you show me a photograph, Mark?' he asked, shaking his head in disbelief. 'Why, so you did! So that's how I know you, Miss Kennedy!'

Tobie inclined her head and smiled, but her mouth was parched, in spite of the coffee. For one awful moment she thought Harvey must have known of her relationship with Robert, or conceivably seen some painting of his that bore her some resemblance.

As if realising he was intruding, Harvey got to his feet then and ambled away, and Mark came round the sofa to take his place. 'Old soak!' he muttered, as he came down beside her. 'Half the time he doesn't even know his own name.'

Tobie endeavoured to act normally. 'He—he seems harmless enough,' she ventured, but Mark only scowled.

'Like I said, he lives on other people. Where would he be without Rob to buy him his life-giving elixir?'

'You mean Robert—subsidises the Jennings?'

'He calls it payment for Cilla's services. Myself, I'd call it something else.'

Tobie shook her head. 'Why are you so bitter? He doesn't live off you.'

'He does—indirectly,' Mark muttered, almost

inaudibly, but at her startled glance he had to elucidate. 'Well, look,' he continued, in an undertone, 'it stands to reason, doesn't it? I mean, we—that is, Mother and I—we're Rob's only family. If anything happened to him, naturally we're his next of kin—'

'*Mark!*'

Tobie's protest was louder than she had intended, and her face coloured as she attracted curious eyes.

Mark, meanwhile, covered her hand with his where it lay on the sofa between them, and added softly: 'We have to be realistic, honey. Unless Rob gets married, I stand to inherit everything, and believe me, I'd have Harvey Jennings off this island so quickly his feet wouldn't even touch the ground!'

Cilla and her father departed around midnight, and Tobie took the opportunity to make good her own escape. Her head was aching quite abominably now, and she badly wanted to be alone. She needed time to assimilate what had been said, and how it affected her, and she wished quite desperately that it was they, and not Robert, who was leaving in the morning.

She said her goodnights and climbed the stairs tiredly, holding on to the balustrade. She felt drained of the confidence that had gripped her earlier in the evening, and even her limbs felt heavy. In her room, she closed the door and leant back against it wearily.

With the windows ajar, moonlight streamed

into the apartment. In its ghostly illumination, the long silk curtains moved like wraiths in the draught, and the rails of the balcony cast a shadow like prison bars across the rug-strewn floor. Was that how she saw the island now—a prison? she wondered despairingly, and felt the unwilling knowledge of her recklessness stir the guilty pain inside her. No matter where she turned, nothing could alter the fact that Robert had paid more heavily than she for his indifference, and the memory of her anger against him lingered only as a dying ember.

Disturbing, too, was Mark's opinion of the future. Did he really expect to outlive Robert, and was that why there had been a reconciliation in the family? It was a harsh assessment, and one she would have discounted before this evening. Could it be conceivable that that was why Mrs Newman was throwing Mark and Cilla together? Because Cilla was the only threat to her otherwise secure existence?

With impatient fingers she took off her gown, tearing the fragile fasteners in her haste. But she wanted to be free of anything associated with the evening's events, and she breathed more easily when the night air eddied coolly about her slim body.

She decided to take a shower, to cleanse her skin of any impurities, and in its icy stream she felt a sense of invigoration. It was no use purging herself for something that was irretrievable. The words had been said; their cruelty could not be withdrawn. And at least Robert could have no idea of the torment they had brought her.

In bed, however, without any other recourse, she could not prevent her thoughts from returning to the essence of what she had learned. Robert—who had taught her everything she knew about the needs of her body, and his—could never make love again, could never hold a girl in his arms and reduce her to a clinging, yielding, eager supplicant. He had been an expert at getting what he wanted, and in her innocence she had had no will to resist him. She loved him, and the miracle had been that he had seemed to love her, too. Certainly their affair had lasted longer than any of his other affairs. For six months he had seen no other woman, and she had learned, through the angry phone calls that had come to the apartment, that this was not usual for him.

Even so, she had been naïve. She had dared to hope that he intended to marry her. He had known he had been the first man with her, and when she became pregnant she hadn't worried too much. It never occurred to her that Robert might think that she would handle that side of things, or that that was why he had never held back. Besides, she defended herself now, in their most passionate moments she doubted he could have done so. He had been too aroused to care about anything but satisfying their mutual needs, filling her with his strength and collapsing exhaustedly beside her. . .

The memories were becoming too painful, and she rolled over on to her stomach, resting her face on her folded arms. If only she had never come here, she thought helplessly, if only she could have gone on hating him and blaming him, and feeling the resentment which had sustained her for so long now. If only. . .

CHAPTER SIX

In spite of her anxieties she must have slept, however, for when she opened her eyes again she realised something—or someone—had awakened her. She lay there in the semi-darkness, her heart pounding heavily in her ears, with the uneasy feeling that she was no longer alone in the room. She couldn't see anything, she couldn't hear anything above the uneven intake of her own breathing, but she was convinced that she was not mistaken. The shadows seemed darker somehow, as if some denser mass was deflecting the moon's silvery light, and she propped herself up on one elbow, reaching for the switch on the lamp beside the bed.

But before she was able to turn the lamp on, the solid shape of a body came between her and the light streaming through the half-open shutters. As a scream rose automatically into her throat, a firm hand covered her mouth, pressing her back against the pillows, as a human weight depressed the springs of the bed beside her.

Panic almost choked her. She fought desperately to free herself from that suffocating mask, threshing about upon the bed like a wild thing, struggling frantically to get herself free. In those first few seconds she gave little thought to the incongruity of her actions, or recognised the impossibility of her intruder being anyone she didn't know. It simply didn't occur to her. She acted completely on impulse, and when her teeth plunged recklessly into the palm that covered her mouth, she was astounded when a familiar voice swore violently before withdrawing the offending member.

Instantly Tobie's aggression sagged, and her limbs went weak. She was so shocked, she could only lie there, gazing up at his shadowy profile, hardly believing what her ears and eyes were telling her was true. He massaged his wounded palm, sitting on the side of the bed, returning her stare with what she felt sure was grim malevolence.

'Robert?' she said at last, when he made no attempt to speak to her. 'Robert, what are you doing here?'

He made no immediate response, and as her eyes accustomed themselves to the shadow she saw he was still wearing the lace-frilled shirt he had worn earlier in the evening, and the close-fitting velvet pants. He had shed his jacket however, and unbuttoned the shirt, and in the aftermath of their battle she could see his chest rising and falling with the quickened pace of his breathing.

Yet, even as her brain acknowledged these things, common sense was returning to her. What was he doing here? she wondered, with a returning sense of panic. Why had he come? And what was she doing, letting him stay here, as if he had that right?

'Please—I think you should go—' she got out
urgently, before his next move caught her off
balance.

He turned then, putting one hand on either side
of her, imprisoning her within the arc of his arms,
looking down at her with an intensity that com-
municated itself even in the darkness. 'Why
should I go?' he demanded huskily. 'I don't want
to go, and I don't believe you really want me to.'

'You're mad!' Tobie knew she had to keep her
head whatever happened. 'I don't know what you
think you're doing, but I can assure you—'

'Yes, I'm sure you can,' he interrupted her
roughly, one hand moving slightly so that the pad
of his thumb brushed the sun-kissed skin of her
upper arm. 'Assure me, I mean. Assure me that
I'm neither insensitive nor impotent. Merely
patient, that's all.'

'Robert, stop this!' She shifted to avoid his
caressing thumb. 'What are you doing here? How
did you get here?' This as the remembrance of
his disability returned to torture her.

'I managed,' he responded, without emphasis,
bending his head so that his tongue replaced
the tormenting invasion of his fingers. 'Hmm,
you taste delicious! All warm, and soft, and
yielding—'

'I'll scream,' she choked, struggling to maintain her calm. 'I—I'll scream—'

'Go ahead,' he taunted, his lips straying across
the exposed bones of her shoulder to the scented
curve of her breast. 'Who will hear you? No one
sleeps in this wing of the house but you. The

family's rooms are well away from here. We're quite alone, quite private—'

Tobie twisted away from his exploring lips, desperation taking the place of disbelief. What was he doing here? Why had he come? Did he know who she was? Did he remember? Or was this evening's fiasco the reason for this incredible intrusion?

'What about Mark?' she got out at last, seizing on the only resort left to her, without revealing herself. 'What about your brother? I thought you cared about him? Surely you would never do anything to hurt him?'

Robert lifted his head, but it was only a moment's respite. She could still see the sensual curve of his mouth, and the mocking glitter of his eyes.

'How can I hurt Mark?' he enquired, to her disbelieving ears. 'Mark need never know. Not unless you tell him, of course.' He paused. 'It's not as if I'm trespassing on virgin territory, is it?' He hesitated again, while she gazed up at him with horrified eyes. 'I mean, Mark told us all about you. About your—affair; and the baby you so conveniently got rid of!'

Tobie's lips parted, but no sound came from them, and before she could say anything in her own defence Robert's mouth covered hers. It was an intimate kiss, and one which she could not ignore, as she had attempted to ignore his earlier caresses. Her parted lips exposed the vulnerable sweetness within, and beneath that disturbing pressure she felt herself weakening. The years between them swept away, as her bones dissolved to water.

Any doubts she might have had, that all feeling had died with her baby, were extinguished. So far as Robert was concerned she was as vulnerable as ever, and as the feeling swelled between them she felt any remaining shreds of detachment torn from her. He seemed aware of it, too, lowering himself on to her, crushing her breasts beneath the weight of his body. He kicked the single sheet, which was all that had covered her, aside and the muscles of his thighs imprisoned hers, the hardness of his legs a disturbing reality. His hands were at her shoulders, forcing the narrow straps of her nightgown to yield, and presently she felt the air cool against her skin.

'Robert, please—' she groaned, when his mouth released hers to find the swollen peaks of her breasts, but when his lips returned to bruise hers once again, she felt herself weakening.

Dear God, she thought desperately, trying to hold on to her sanity, what did he think she was? Why was he doing this? What motive did he have? And how could she ask, without betraying herself? Was it only what she had said? And what did he know about the baby? What had Mark told him?

His mouth strayed lower over the creamy skin of her midriff as he tore the shred of nightgown from her, exposing her slender form to his gaze. Even in those moments of extreme tension, Tobie felt herself surrendering beneath his eyes, her limbs quivering with emotion as he surveyed her yielding shape. It was becoming increasingly difficult to separate the two parts of her life, the two men she had known as Robert Lang; and to her eternal shame she knew an urgent desire to fuse the two halves into one. Indeed, she was hard pressed not to put her arms around his neck and pull that urgent mouth back to hers, assuage the hunger only he was capable of arousing. It was only the knowledge that he was doing this for reasons other than any she understood that compelled her to go on resisting him, when every nerve and sinew in her body wanted to respond.

'Tell me about the men in your life, Tobie,' Robert said now, drawing back to look down at her, his eyes dark and enigmatic. 'Tell me about the father of your child. The child you so badly wanted to be rid of.'

Tobie stared at him in mortification. He had kissed her and caressed her, exposed her naked body to his gaze, and now he chose to indulge in idle conversation. Or was it idle conversation? What was at the bottom of it? Why was he doing this?

'Why does that interest you?' she countered now, without answering him. 'What kind of man are you? You can lie here with your brother's girl-friend—'

'My *half*-brother's girl-friend,' he contradicted her harshly. 'Let's be accurate, shall we?' His lips twisted. 'And to return to my question—'

'Why should I answer you?' she cried, trying without success to wrest the sheet and cover herself. 'I don't see what—what my affairs have to do with you!'

'*Affairs* being the operative word, I assume,' he observed contemptuously, and she caught her breath.

'What—what did Mark tell you about me?'

'What did Mark—' He broke off abruptly. 'Why, what would you expect him to tell his loving family? Only that the girl he cares about— the girl he hopes to marry—first became known to him on the operating table!'

Tobie bit her lips to prevent them from trembling. 'He—told you that?'

Robert inclined his head. 'Mark's essentially an—honest person.' He moved his shoulders indifferently. 'Some might call it weakness. Whatever, our mother is adept at getting to the core of a situation.'

Tobie licked her lips. 'He told you—that was how we met?' she ventured, trying to calculate what this might have meant to Robert, and he nodded again.

'Eventually. My mother wormed it out of him. As I've said, she's an inquisitive woman. She wanted to know all about you. He confessed that originally you'd been his patient. That you'd been brought into the hospital, in a state of some distress. That you'd conveniently lost the child you were carrying—'

'Conveniently?' Tobie broke in, apprehensive, yet desperate enough to welcome the truth.

'Conveniently, yes.' Robert was not disturbed. 'You weren't married, it was obvious you wouldn't want the child. So—'

'You think I did it deliberately?' Tobie was appalled. 'I *miscarried*!' She took an uneven breath. 'Something happened—and I miscarried! That was what happened. Nothing else.'

Robert's mouth was a hard line. 'If you insist.' But clearly he did not believe her. 'In any case, Mark was quick to explain that you were in no state to welcome his attentions then. However, you're a beautiful girl, as I'm sure you are aware, and I expect he told you he could not get you out of his mind. It was nothing short of fate that brought you together again that evening at the Albert Hall. Your mutual love of Grieg's music, eyes meeting across a crowded foyer.' His mouth curled. 'And you've been lovers ever since—'

'*No!*' The word burst from Tobie's throat. 'No,' she said again. 'Not—not lovers, never lovers!'

His scepticism was painful, his contempt for her almost tangible. He looked down at her, his features contorted with disbelief, and she shrank beneath the scornful blast of his eyes.

'Do you deny you were attracted to him as he was attracted to you?'

'No—'

'And do you deny that from that evening—how long ago was it?—eighteen months?—you've been constant companions?'

'No.' Tobie shifted restlessly. 'We've been friends—'

'*Friends*!'

'Yes, friends!' Tobie paused. 'In any case, it's

nothing to do with you, is it?' she challenged him in a whisper. 'Mark and I—we live our own lives.'

'Not exactly.' Robert spoke savagely. 'Mark does as he's told, as you've no doubt discovered by now.'

'What are you implying?'

Robert snorted. 'Mark is easily led. Were either I or my mother to forbid Mark to see you again, I've no doubt he'd protest, but he'd do it.'

'I don't believe you.'

Robert shrugged. 'That's your prerogative.'

Tobie moved her head from side to side on the pillow. 'Why are you doing this?' she pleaded, once again. 'What does it matter to you?' She ventured to look at him. 'You don't know me!'

Robert's lashes veiled the expression in his eyes. 'No,' he conceded, after a few moments. 'But I know of you. And what I know doesn't fill me with confidence.'

Tobie gasped. 'What do you think you are? Mark's keeper? Or simply the *seigneur* practising his *droit*?'

Robert's eyes narrowed. 'A tantalising idea, you'll admit.'

Tobie felt too drained to argue any longer. 'So what do you want of me?' she whispered. 'What are you doing here? Why don't you go away and leave me alone? You've told me what you think of me? You've shown me your contempt. You've hurt and humiliated me—'

'Have I done all those things?' Robert interrupted her harshly. 'Have I really? And how do you think I felt this evening when you implied I was of no use to a woman?'

Tobie gasped. 'Is that what all this is about?'

'And if it was?'

'Like I said before—you're mad!' She turned her head sideways on the pillow. 'Oh, please, go away! Just go away!'

'Poor Tobie!'

The alteration in his tone brought her head up with a start. Where before there had been anger and condemnation, suddenly there was tenderness and understanding, and she trusted him no more now than she had done before.

'Poor Tobie,' he said again, his lips softening into indulgence, and the flickering flame of anxiety was rekindled inside her. 'So innocent! So falsely accused! And yet you succumbed to Mark's attentions without a shred of hesitation!'

These last words were said with a return to the harshness he had exhibited before, and Tobie sought to defend herself. 'That's not true,' she protested. 'After—after what happened, I avoided contact with any man for a long time. Even— even when I met Mark that evening, when he invited me out, I refused—'

'But not for long.'

'We became friends, I tell you. Though why I should tell you this, I don't honestly know.'

'Don't you, Tobie? Don't you?'

She stared up into his dark face, wishing she could read his mind. What were his thoughts? What was he thinking? Was his anger really born out of resentment for what she had said, or was

this some sophisticated game of cat and mouse?
Could he have come here if he hadn't known who
she was? Was he really so contemptuous of her
character that he believed she would not tell Mark
what he had done?

What had he done?

The silence between them grew. To Tobie, the
atmosphere seemed charged with electricity, but
she was incapable of doing anything about it. She
was waiting, like prey in the claws of the hunter,
for him to make the next move.

'You know why I came, Tobie, don't you?' he
demanded, at last, when her nerves felt as taut as
violin strings, and she could only shake her head.
'I came to drink at the fountain of your youth, to
worship at the temple of your beauty——'

'No!'

'Why not, Tobie?' He lowered his head to tease
the pulse beating erratically at her throat with his
tongue. 'It's what I want, it's what I need! Like
you, I need to prove something, and unlike you
I can do it.'

'No! No, you mustn't——'

Tobie's frantic efforts to hold him off were
futile. He was so much stronger for one thing,
and his assault was not only a physical one. She
was fighting both him and herself, trying helplessly to suppress the emotions he was arousing
within her. What truth now in the things Mark
had said, in the jealous words she had uttered?
Robert was not impotent, whatever his brother
believed, and all the old memories came flooding
back to weaken her. She couldn't deny the aching

yearning that filled her arching body; she couldn't control her hands when they crept up to his face, her fingers curving around his nape, threading through the heavy darkness of his hair; and she couldn't escape the certain knowledge that she wanted him to make love to her, to invade the silken sheath of her body, that no other man had ever known.

His mouth played with hers, rubbing against her lips, coaxing them to part. His fingers cupped the fullness of her breast, before sliding possessively down over her ribcage to the warm invitation of her thighs. The fine dark hair on his chest was rough against her softness, and she pressed herself closer to the sensuous velvet of his pants, that was all that separated her from the thrusting muscles between his legs. Beneath his experienced lips and hands she was as helpless as a baby, and she gave up the fight without fear of surrender.

'Robert—' she breathed, winding her arms around his neck, but the oath he spoke then was not polite. Even though his mouth clung to hers for several seconds after his crude profanity, his intentions were clear when he tore her arms from him and jack-knifed off the bed.

'No, by God!' he swore, backing away from her and raking back his hair with unsteady hands. And then, as he regained a little more of his equanimity, he added: 'No, Tobie, you're not going to have that satisfaction. I didn't come here to make love to you, even though you obviously thought I did. I came to seduce you, but not to intimacy, only to this—this unwelcome state of distraction. And I think I've succeeded.'

Tobie raised herself on her elbows, her hair in wild disorder, her attitude one of unknowing provocation. Her expression mirrored her shocked bewilderment, and in those first few moments she thought little of pride or dignity.

'Robert, what are you saying?' she cried, stretching out her hand towards him. 'Robert, please—don't go! I—I—'

'Shut up! *Shut up!*'

He turned his back on her then, as if he couldn't bear to look at her, and his awkward movements seemed to bring everything back into focus. In horror, she remembered where they were and what he had said, and when her eyes lowered to the shameless nakedness of her body, she uttered a little groan before she gathered the sheets about her, and buried her hot humiliated face in the pillows.

She didn't hear him go. He left as silently as he had arrived, but when she lifted her head and found herself alone, she felt no sense of reprieve. On the contrary, she felt worse now than she had done that awful day when Robert had slammed out of his apartment, leaving her, had she known it, to face three barren years. Those years were over now, inasmuch as she had met him again, spent time with him again, learned to love him again, if she had ever stopped; but what had gone between could never be retrieved, and whatever his reasons for punishing her, she was left in no doubt that he despised her and everything she stood for.

With a feeling of intense weariness Tobie got off the bed now, not bothering to put on her nightgown again. The burning heat of her abasement needed no artificial complement, and she welcomed the coolness that flooded into the room when she opened the balcony doors. Outside, the sky was fractionally lightening, and the greyness before the dawn matched her melancholic mood. She wished she could go to sleep, and wake up far from this serpentine paradise, whose outward appearance was merely a façade hiding the corruption beneath. She wished she need never meet either Robert or his family again, and she knew the craziest impulse to plunge into the sea and swim into oblivion.

A movement below startled her, and she instinctively drew back from the balcony rail. Yet in spite of herself, her eyes were drawn to the tall lean figure that emerged from the shadow of the terrace. Robert, for it was no one else, walked with difficulty down the shallow flight of steps that led to the gardens. He *walked*, Tobie saw with reluctant admiration. Not easily, it was true: but without sticks, a slow, sometimes awkward tread, that revealed that his condition was by no means as hopeless as Mark and his mother believed.

Watching him, Tobie felt the tears building up behind her eyes. It was hopeless, she thought devastatedly. No matter what he did, no matter how he treated her, she loved him, and she would have given everything she possessed to be able to give him back the years that he had lost.

She was awakened by a hammering on her door.

Heavy-eyed, she dragged the sheet over her nakedness, and groped for the clock on the table beside her. She couldn't believe it. It was after eleven o'clock! She had slept almost eight hours!

'Tobie! Tobie, are you there? Can I come in?'

It was Mark's voice, and immediately Tobie felt the hot colour sweep into her cheeks once more. How could she face him? How could she face any of them? She had betrayed everything she thought she believed in, and she dreaded the censure she was sure must follow.

Swallowing hard, she called: 'Yes. Yes, you can come in!' and tucked the sheet securely round her, imprisoning it sarongwise beneath her arms.

The door opened and Mark appeared, his fair, good-looking face mirroring his impatience. 'Well!' he declared, surveying her recumbent state with some disapproval. 'Do you know what time it is?'

'Yes.' Tobie put up a nervous hand to her hair. 'I'm sorry, I——I must have overslept.'

'Overslept!' Mark was scornful. 'We thought perhaps you were ill or something. You've slept almost *twelve* hours!'

'No. I mean——well, no, I haven't really.' Tobie chose her words carefully. 'I——as a matter of fact, I didn't sleep much before dawn.' She shrugged. 'Over-excited, I suppose.' It was an understatement. 'I'm sorry.' More sorry than he could ever know.

Mark sniffed, shoving his hands into the pockets of his shorts. 'Well? Are you going to get up now? Or would you like Monique to bring you breakfast—'

'Heavens, no! Tobie shook her head vigorously. I—I—of course, I'll get up right away. But don't worry about breakfast. I'm not hungry.'

Mark squared his shoulders. 'Nevertheless, you've got to have something,' he stated doggedly. 'I had enough of Rob, taking me to task last week, when you missed out on lunch and made yourself ill. You have to have something in this climate. I'll get Monique to make some coffee. We can share it by the pool, if you like.'

'Thank you.' But Tobie's response was absent. So Robert had chastised Mark for not looking after her. *So what*?

'Right, I'll leave you to get dressed, then,' Mark said now, without making any attempt to touch her. 'I should warn you, Mother's in no fit state herself this morning, so don't do anything to annoy her, will you?'

'Oh!' Tobie's stomach plunged. Surely Robert's mother hadn't observed her son's visit to their guest's rooms last night. Surely that wasn't the reason for her indisposition.

'I guess it's Rob, as usual,' Mark added, unknowingly answering her question. 'He and Cilla leaving for Miami like that, without even saying goodbye.'

Tobie's shoulders sagged. *Of course*! How

could she have been so stupid? Robert and Cilla were leaving for Miami this morning. For a few moments she had forgotten it. For a few moments she had been anticipating meeting him again. But now it all swam into perspective. Last night's visit could not have been better planned. Robert's departure this morning ensured that she should not have the opportunity of taxing him with his duplicity, and by the time he returned, she and Mark would be getting ready to leave. If indeed she could wait that long before escaping from this impossible situation. . .

'They—they've gone?' she asked now, unnecessarily, aware of Mark's speculative gaze, and he nodded.

'Early,' he agreed. 'Jim Matheson picked them up. Mother is furious. But like I told her, Rob never would respond to coercion.'

'Coercion?' Tobie echoed faintly, and Mark nodded again.

'Last night, after you'd gone to bed. After Cilla and her father had gone home. Mother put it to him that he was doing no good, encouraging Cilla, that he had no right to let her think he might marry her. Rob's not going to marry anybody. Like I told you, he's not a well man. He needs peace and tranquillity to work, something to sustain his interest. Not the trials and tribulations of a relationship that could never be more than platonic.'

Tobie almost choked, but she managed to change it into a cough before saying: 'How—how do you know that? Why do you say—Robert's impotent? How can you be so sure?'

Mark shrugged. 'It's the paralysis,' he explained, half impatiently. 'By now, if there was going to be any marked improvement, it would have been evident. He should have been on his feet, walking; but you've seen him. He can barely drag himself across the floor on those two sticks. God knows how he manages to dress and undress himself. It must be a constant battle. But he won't let anyone help him. He insists he can manage. Only his physician knows the whole truth, of course, but having spoken to him, I'm not optimistic.'

Tobie shook her head. She could have told him that Robert could walk. She could have told him that the improvement he had looked for was there. But for some reason she didn't. Just as she had never betrayed Robert's early morning swim in the pool, or his independence of the sticks she had first noticed at his studio that day. She didn't know why she felt this need to respect his confidence. Certainly it was not through any respect he had for her. But, in spite of everything, she knew he had his reasons for keeping his real condition to himself, and having denied him so much, she could not take that away from him.

'Anyway,' Mark went on now, 'there's no point in wishing things were different. Rob's disabled. That's all there is to it. And it's to be hoped he comes to his senses before submitting Cilla to the kind of life she would be forced to lead with him.'

Tobie licked her dry lips. 'Perhaps Cilla

wouldn't mind,' she ventured, but Mark only snorted.

'Cilla's a woman, like other women,' he declared. 'She may think otherwise now, but sooner or later she'll want more. She'll want children, a real family. And that's something Rob can't give her.'

Tobie hesitated, and then she said deliberately: 'They could adopt a child——'only to break off in shocked surprise when Mark uncharacteristically swore at her.

'Adopt a child!' He went on angrily. 'Don't be so bloody stupid! They can't adopt a child! My mother wouldn't want some snotty-nosed kid who wasn't even her grandchild running about Soledad! There are valuable things here—china, porcelain, paintings! Why, the house is a veritable goldmine! Do you think we would stand for somebody else's bastard inheriting Emerald Cay? You must be out of your mind!' And with a gesture of frustration he stormed out of the room.

Tobie remained where she was several minutes after the door had banged behind him. It was incredible, but until then she had not known Mark had a temper. She supposed it was unnatural to think that he might not have one, particularly as his mother and brother exhibited theirs so freely, but Mark had always seemed so meek, somehow, so biddable, and to find herself facing an implacable force seemed totally alien to her.

Nevertheless, nothing could alter the fact that so far as Mark and his mother were concerned, Emerald Cay was their home, and they obviously

intended to keep it that way. She wondered for
the first time if they really cared about Robert at
all, except as a provider. Could it possibly be true
that his words to her, which had seemed so cyni-
cal at the time, had some basis in fact? Had his
mother only effected a reconciliation after the
accident because she suspected he was going to
die? It was ghoulish, but after listening to Mark
she had to consider it. Was his mother's only
reason for living here a way of ensuring her
younger son an inheritance? Did she really care
so little for Robert?

Tobie felt shaken as she got out of bed. What
a tangled coil it was, she thought sickly, and she
had contributed to it by coming here. If only she
could leave now, today, before anything else happened. And yet, deep inside her, she knew an
almost pathological desire to stay and witness
their astonishment when Robert revealed the
truth.

CHAPTER SEVEN

ROBERT and Cilla returned three days later.

Tobie was sunbathing beside the pool when she saw the Cessna circling the island prior to landing, and her skin prickled uneasily at the prospect of their eventual encounter. She didn't know what to expect of him, how he intended to treat her. And only stubbornness, and determination, and a kind of wilful masochism, kept her from making for the comparative sanctuary of Mark's presence.

Mark was indoors, helping his mother with her correspondence. During the past couple of days he had spent a lot of time with his mother, and his embarrassment at neglecting Tobie was painfully evident. Yet, for all that, he seemed incapable of refusing his mother anything, and Tobie thought how fortunate it was that she was not desperately in love with Mark. She doubted the situation would have been any different, and with uncharacteristic cynicism she acknowledged that even love would have faltered under such duress.

In the circumstances, it had proved providential. The last thing she wanted now was Mark making some concerted assault on her emotions. Much better if they could complete their holiday without any distressing scene, and back in London it would be easier to make the break. It was strange how living with someone day to day revealed traits in their make-up one had hitherto not observed. Living with Robert had been like that, too, but whereas Mark had displayed a weakness in his character she had not suspected, Robert had proved stronger than both of them.

Living with Robert. . .

Resting back on her elbows, Tobie allowed her thoughts to drift. She remembered how shocked Laura had been when she had told her sister what she intended to do. Laura's world only encompassed engagements and marriage, diamond rings and orange blossom—she could not understand her younger sister's determination to share an apartment with a man who had not even mentioned a permanent commitment.

She had tried to dissuade her. Her husband Dave, Tobie's brother-in-law, had even gone to see Robert, much to Tobie's mortification, and demanded to know what his game was. Somehow Robert had convinced him he was not the lecherous brute they imagined. Indeed, on occasion Laura and Dave had had dinner with them at the apartment, but once Tobie knew she was pregnant, things had started to go wrong.

She sighed now, rolling on to her stomach, exposing the honey-tanned skin of her back to the sun. Had she been so naïve? Why had she forced the issue like that? She should have known Robert was not someone one could force into anything. What had Mark said? He didn't respond to coercion? That was true. And she supposed her clumsy efforts to make her feelings known had sounded like coercion to him.

She circled her lips with her tongue. What might have happened if Robert hadn't had his accident? Would things have been different? If she had not had to suffer the humiliation of being turned away from the hospital. If she had known he had suffered amnesia. . .

She cupped her chin on one hand. Who had been responsible for denying her access to his presence? she wondered. Who had announced that he didn't want to see her? Who had made that cruel statement, which had aroused such desperation inside her that she had lost the baby? It couldn't have been Robert, she realised, with sudden insight, not if he had been as broken up as he said. So who had driven her away from the hospital, and into Mark's professional hands?

The sound of a car engine in the courtyard below precluded her speculation, and presently she heard the whisper of Robert's chair wheels being propelled up the slope to the patio. With sudden nervousness she sat up, crossing her legs half defensively, belatedly aware of the scant protection offered by the dark brown bikini.

Cilla was wheeling his chair, her small face flushed and vivacious, as if she was well pleased with life. For once she was wearing a skirt instead of shorts, and her lime green shirt was made of the same ribbed cotton.

Robert, as usual, wore denim, his shirt open at the neck to expose the tanned column of his throat. He, too, appeared in the best of spirits, although there were lines of weariness around his eyes, as if, Tobie thought jealously, he had been burning the candle at both ends.

Avoiding his eyes, she looked first at Cilla's hands, or more particularly at the third finger of her left hand, and her relief when she saw no ring there was almost palpable. At least Robert had not taken the opportunity to get engaged while he was in Miami, though it was possible he had bought a ring and was waiting to ask Harvey's permission.

'Tobie.'

He was acknowledging her now, and with an effort she forced herself to respond. 'Wel-welcome home,' she got out jerkily, the words almost choking her, and she saw the sardonic compression of his mouth.

She hoped Cilla would not notice how quickly she was breathing, or how difficult it was to control the colour in her face. But nothing could prevent her awareness of the last time Robert had seen her, and the memory of his cruelty was impossible to erase. How could she love someone who continually hurt her, she wondered, while her eyes searched his face for some sign of compassion. And why should he assume her complicity, when she knew now she had nothing to lose?

'We've had a marvellous time!' Cilla chose that moment to make her own contribution. 'We haven't had a free minute, Tobie, honestly. It's been really tremendous!'

'I'm so pleased.' Tobie's words sounded stiff, even to her ears, but with Robert's eyes upon her, assessing her every move, it was impossible to relax. With an unknowingly graceful movement she got to her feet, reaching for the protection of a towel and adding: 'Would you like me to order you some tea?'

'Not for me.' Robert's refusal was abrupt. 'What I want most is a shower and a change of clothes. If you'll both excuse me. . .'

Tobie stood aside obediently as he propelled his chair towards the open windows, and then, aware that Cilla was looking at her, she turned to the girl, forcing a smile.

'How about you?' she suggested, moving her shoulders enquiringly. 'Or are you in a hurry to get home?'

'Oh, no.' Cilla lounged casually on to the swing couch. 'Robert's eating with us tonight, so I'll just wait for him. But if you want some tea, I'll share it with you.'

It was not what Tobie wanted at all. She felt a curious resentment that Robert should choose to dine with the Jennings on his first night home, and her antagonism towards the other girl made her feel quite sick. She knew the craziest impulse to tell Cilla about her and Robert, to wipe that smug expression from her face once and for all. But instead she nodded politely, summoned Monique, and sustained her composure until Mark appeared.

'Hey, you're back!' he exclaimed, greeting Cilla with evident pleasure. 'I thought I heard the plane. Where's Rob?'

'He's gone to change,' replied Cilla easily,

making room for him to join her on the couch. 'Tobie's ordered some tea. Why don't you join us?'

'I'll do that.' Mark's enthusiasm began to irritate Tobie. 'What could be nicer than sharing afternoon tea with two beautiful girls? I'd better make the most of it before Rob comes back.'

Cilla laughed, and Tobie turned to stare broodingly down towards the harbour. She felt tense and disorientated, and fleetingly wondered whether she might not be suffering from a mild sunstroke. It would be nice to think she could find physical reasons for her physical and emotional condition, but somehow she doubted it.

'Did you have a good time, then?' Mark was asking now, and Tobie thought, rather spitefully, that Cilla had only been waiting for such an opportunity.

'Oh, we had a wonderful time!' she assured him eagerly. 'We stayed in this fantastic hotel at Bal Harbour, and we ate in a different restaurant every night. We went to a casino one evening, and do you know, I won over two hundred dollars! Isn't that incredible? I spent it all the next day on the most beautiful evening gown you've ever seen. I've bought heaps of things, clothes, and souvenirs. I bought Daddy a new pipe and some tobacco, and Robert insisted on adding a bottle of his favourite cognac.'

The arrival of Monique with the tray of tea concluded this monologue, much to Tobie's relief. She had the maid set the tray on a low table beside her own chair, and took charge of its distribution with real enthusiasm. Even Mrs Newman's appearance did not interrupt her concentration, even when the older woman looked askance at her informal attire.

'So you're home, Cilla,' Mrs Newman remarked, in somewhat cool tones. 'I didn't hear Henri leave with the car.'

'He didn't,' said Cilla, a little uncomfortably now. 'We used the Mini.'

'Ah, yes. As you did the morning you left,' Mark's mother observed acidly. 'I'm surprised at you, Cilla. You didn't even say goodbye.'

Cilla licked her lips. 'We left very early, Mrs Newman,' she averred defensively. 'Robert didn't want to disturb you.'

'I'm well aware of my son's propensity for discourtesy—however, I had thought better of you, Cilla,' the older woman persisted coldly, and to her surprise, Tobie's sympathies were with the girl now.

'I expect Cilla was too excited at the prospect of the trip,' she interposed lightly, earning a grateful smile. 'Why don't you ask her whether she enjoyed herself? As they're home safely, it doesn't really matter how they left, does it?'

'When I want your opinion, Tobie, I shall ask for it,' Mrs Newman declared sharply, switching her attention to her. 'And just as a point of interest, one doesn't normally serve tea in a bikini.'

'Why? Because it runs through the holes?' enquired a dry voice behind them, and Cilla giggled uncontrollably in a release of tension.

'Of course, I would expect a remark like that

from you, Robert,' his mother commented bleakly, as her son wheeled his chair into their midst. 'Do I take it you endorse Miss Kennedy's appearance? I'm not sure Cilla would appreciate that any more than I do.'

Tobie's face burned, Mark looked uncomfortable, and Cilla assumed an embarrassed silence. It was only in the aftermath that Tobie realised how cleverly Mrs Newman had manipulated the situation. By drawing everyone's attention to Robert's apparent approval of Tobie's provocative appearance, she had successfully alienated all of them, and created an atmosphere charged with emotion.

'Any man worth the name would appreciate Tobie's appearance.' Robert responded now without reticence. 'Wouldn't you agree, Mark?'

'What? Oh—yes.' Mark shifted awkwardly in his seat, more susceptible to his mother's censorious gaze. 'Of course.' He made an apologetic gesture, although to whom Tobie could not be quite sure. 'Eh—Tobie knows how I feel,' he finished ambiguously.

Tobie said nothing. Instead, she concentrated on the fragile china cup in her hands, unwilling to get any further involved in family conflict, and Cilla, recovering from her embarrassment, said:

'I think Tobie looks jolly nice. I wish I looked as good in a bikini.'

'Oh, well—obviously I'm old-fashioned.' With tightened lips Mrs Newman endeavoured to retire unscathed, but Robert had other ideas.

'I don't agree, Mother,' he remarked, helping

himself to a sandwich from the tray. 'Old-fashioned—that evokes an image of old-world charm and humour, of integrity and loyalty, and faithfulness; marriage vows, silly little things that used to mean something. Oh, no—' He paused, and Tobie saw the condemnation in his eyes and was chilled by it. 'I wouldn't call you old-fashioned, Mother. You had no time for such trivia in your youth, as we all know.'

'Rob, honestly!'

'Robert!'

Mark's indignant ejaculation just preceded the cry that issued from Cilla's lips, and Mrs Newman's face froze. Only Tobie was not truly shocked by what he had said. On the contrary, remembering the antagonism between them, she was surprised it had not flared up before this. And while she could sympathise with his mother's humiliation, she could not deny that Mrs Newman had brought this upon herself.

Mark had sprung to his feet to go to his mother's side, however, and now he turned on his brother angrily. 'Can't you let that old history remain dead and buried, Rob?' he demanded, putting a reassuring arm about his mother's shoulders. 'My God! You didn't suffer by it. You were too young. And Mother saw that you were well cared for. Why don't you just forget it?'

'Forget my father's death, you mean?' asked Robert, with deceptive mildness, and Mark's chin jutted, accentuating the differences between them.

'My father's dead, too, remember?' he retorted, while Tobie wished the ground would open up and swallow her. 'And I don't blame Mother for it.'

'Your father didn't choke his guts out on the end of a piece of wire,' replied Robert succinctly, throwing the remains of his sandwich on to the tray. 'If he had, you might have viewed the situation entirely differently.'

'You bastard!' Mark's pale features contorted. 'If your old man was half as objectionable as you are, I'm not surprised Mother walked out on him—'

Robert's uncoiling from the chair was as swift as it was deadly, and his long fingers curled violently around the collar of Mark's shirt, almost choking him. 'You'll take that back!' he said, with cold malevolence, and only Tobie had the courage to intervene.

Springing to her feet, she came between them, and it was to Robert she instinctively turned. 'For goodness' sake,' she exclaimed, meeting his incensed gaze with appealing insistence, 'can't you both remember you have guests in the house?'

Robert stared at her broodingly for several seconds, and she trembled beneath that penetrating appraisal. So had he looked at her before he stormed out of the apartment three years ago, and time stretched as he continued to fight her. But when she put a tentative hand on his chest, his grip on his brother eased, and Mark took the opportunity to drag himself away, tugging at his collar and massaging his reddening flesh.

'Yes.' It was Mrs Newman who had spoken,

and Tobie had to steel herself to turn and face the other woman. 'Yes, you boys must stop brawling,' their mother continued, almost as if it had been as simple as that. 'Mark, I think you should apologise to Robert for speaking as you did, and Robert, you must try and control that temper of yours. You were always an impulsive boy, acting without thinking. We all have our personal memories of the past to haunt us, but I'm sure after all I've done for you, you don't really bear me a grudge.'

Tobie moved away as Robert sank back into his chair. He seemed exhausted by events, and Cilla came to him at once, asking if there was anything he wanted. Mark, for his part, grumbled but complied, and Tobie was sickened anew when she heard his obedient words of apology. In spite of everything, life would apparently go on as before, and as soon as she could she made her escape, seeking the solace of her own room.

The fact that Robert had arranged to join the Jennings for dinner proved to be a godsend. Tobie did not see how they could have all sat around a table together, so soon after the things that had been said, and instead only she, Mark and his mother shared the long table in the dining room.

Even so, it was not an enjoyable meal. Mrs Newman was evidently brooding over Tobie's contribution to the scene that had erupted, and despite her mild words earlier she was by no means appeased. Whatever she had said to Robert, whatever impression she had created for

Cilla's benefit, she obviously blamed Tobie for what had happened, and even Mark seemed morose and uncommunicative.

'When do you leave, darling?'

Mrs Newman addressed her son after dismissing Monique's offer to serve the coffee, and Tobie tensed at the thought of their anticipated departure.

'The day after tomorrow,' Mark responded now, confirming what Tobie already expected. 'We fly back to Castries, as we did on the way out, but our flight leaves the same evening, so we'll be back in London the next morning.'

'Two days.' His mother shook her head regretfully. 'Your holiday's passed so quickly. I seem to have seen nothing of you.'

Mark glanced significantly at Tobie before looking at his mother again. 'We've had quite a lot of time together, Mother,' he protested. 'And it won't be long before I'm back again.'

'Christmas!' said Mrs Newman impatiently. 'Mark, that's five months away! Oh,' she sighed, 'if only you lived here!'

Tobie bent her head. It was evident what Mrs Newman really meant. She wished Mark lived at Soledad instead of Robert, and her indignation swelled when Mark exclaimed:

'If only Rob would agree to setting up that clinic in Castries! I'd only be a short flight away, and you could come and stay with me.'

His mother nodded. 'Of course, that would be ideal.' She shook her head. 'But you won't get anywhere if you repeat that scene this afternoon.'

Tobie hid her incredulity as Mark nodded, propping his head on one hand. 'I know, I know. But you didn't think I was going to let him get away with that, did you? Sarcastic swine! I could have knocked his teeth down his throat!'

Mrs Newman stretched out her hand and squeezed his arm. 'I understand, darling. But I don't bruise that easily. Robert's father couldn't hurt me, and neither can his son. Relax, I can handle Robert.'

Tobie abruptly pushed back her chair and got to her feet. 'I'm going for a walk,' she announced through stiff lips, and without waiting for any-one's permission, she left the room.

Outside, the night air was blessedly cool and clean, after the cloying atmosphere that sur-rounded the Newmans. She was past caring what they thought of her behaviour. She just knew she had to get out of the house, and she took several gulps of air before descending the steps to the courtyard below.

Since she had come to Emerald Cay her whole world seemed to have been turned on its head. Everything had seemed so clean-cut, back in London. She liked Mark, she enjoyed his com-panionship, and she thought she loved him. The fact that he was Robert's half-brother had played some part in her attraction towards him, she could not deny that, but after what had happened— or rather, what she thought had happened—she expected to feel only contempt when they met. Indeed, she had anticipated their meeting with a certain amount of satisfaction, and she had intended to exploit her relationship with Mark to the hilt.

Looking back on her thoughts now, she realised how foolish they had been. What she had deluded herself was contempt was in fact jealousy, and had Robert been the same man she had first fallen in love with, she doubted she would have survived so long. She dreaded to think what a fool of herself she would have made if he had been his old arrogant self, sweeping aside her shield of detachment and making her see how she really felt. What price now her fine boast of self-assurance, the protection she thought Mark's love would give her? Faced with reality, she would not have stood a chance, and only Robert's amnesia had saved her.

Yet 'saved' her was not perhaps the most suitable word. His physical disability had created doubts more painful than she could have imagined. It had altered the situation so completely, she had been cast adrift on an uncharted sea, facing dangers she had not anticipated, finding emotion her only weapon. What did Robert want of her? Why had he humiliated her so? And how much did he remember of those months before the crash?

'Tobie. . .'

The unexpected use of her name brought her round with a start, her heart pounding in her ears enough to deafen her. In the light reflected from the fountain that tumbled into its stone basin, she saw that Mark had come to join her, and knew an unwelcome sense of anticlimax as he came to stand beside her.

'I've been looking for you,' he said, pushing his hands deep into the pockets of his jacket. 'Mother's gone to bed. She wasn't feeling very well, and I thought you and I should have a talk.'

'Oh, yes?'

Tobie tried to sound casual, and Mark nodded. 'Yes,' he confirmed, gesturing towards the steps, and they began to climb together. 'Mother told me something before dinner that I found rather disquieting, and I wanted to speak to you about it.'

Tobie's mouth felt dry. She couldn't imagine what Mrs Newman might have said to cause Mark to look so solemn, and she sought about desperately in her mind for a solution.

'It has to do with Rob,' Mark went on, and Tobie stiffened.

'Rob—Robert?'

'That's right.' Mark sighed, glancing sideways at her. 'She told me that she believes you knew Rob before you came here.' He paused, and when Tobie didn't immediately say anything, he went on: 'She says she's almost sure she's seen a portrait of you in Rob's studio.'

Tobie's face flooded with colour, but fortunately the moonlight protected her. However, he was waiting for an answer, and somehow she had to give him one.

'When—when did she decide this?' she asked, playing for time, and Mark reluctantly explained. 'It was that night—the night the Jennings ate

with us. She overheard old Harvey asking if he
could have seen you somewhere, and it alerted a
chord in her memory.'

Tobie could have said that Mrs Newman had
waited long enough before voicing her doubts.
But perhaps she had known all along. Certainly
Tobie had had that feeling. And now, two nights
before they were due to leave, she was prepared
to sow the seeds of suspicion in Mark's mind.
Perhaps she thought Tobie would lie to him. It
would obviously be easier, and then later his
mother could expose her for the liar she
undoubtedly was. But why create such a situation,
particularly after the row Mark and Robert had
just had?

'Well?' Mark was waiting. 'Is it true? Does
Rob have a picture of you in his studio?'

Tobie sighed. 'I don't know, do I?'

'Perhaps I should have said, *could* he have a
picture of you in his studio?' Mark corrected himself harshly. 'Tobie, has Rob painted you?'

Tobie licked her lips. 'You mean—before I
came here?'

'You know what I mean.'

Tobie sighed. 'Yes.'

Mark stopped to stare at her. 'You mean—you
and Rob—'

'I mean I knew Robert in London some years
ago.' Tobie shook her head. 'But he doesn't
remember.'

'What do you mean?' Mark was sceptical.

'I mean he's forgotten. It's true. I wouldn't lie
to you.'

Mark's eyes narrowed. 'What do you mean? You didn't tell me you knew Rob.'

'You didn't ask me,' said Tobie evenly.

'But how—what—'

'Does it matter?' Tobie moved her shoulders wearily.

'Of course it matters.' Mark's anger had not subsided. 'My God! And you let me think you were such an innocent!'

Tobie gasped. 'What's that supposed to mean?'

Mark's lips twisted. 'I know my brother. I know what kind of reputation he had before the accident. He wouldn't be content as I was to wait before he got you into his bed!'

Tobie raised her hand to slap his sneering face, and then let it fall. Why should she feel so resentful of his words? They were true. Robert had seduced her—and she had let him.

'Well?' Mark was furious. 'I'm right, aren't I? I can see it in your face. And you'd have married me without telling me!'

'*No!*'

Tobie was adamant now, and he stared at her suspiciously. 'What do you mean—no? I haven't heard this before. If it hadn't been for Mother—'

'I mean, no. No, I'm not going to marry you, Mark,' declared Tobie firmly. 'I never said I would. You only assumed it.'

Mark was open-mouthed. 'But—but—this holiday—'

'—was intended to be just that,' said Tobie quietly. 'And I'm grateful—'

'Grateful!' Mark was shouting now. 'You let me bring you out here, spend money on you—'

'I'll pay you back,' said Tobie unsteadily, straightening her shoulders. 'If you'll let me know how much the air fare—'

'How can you pay me back for staying here?' he demanded shrilly. 'This is a private island. My mother's home—'

'And Robert's, too,' Tobie was stung to respond. 'And as your mother keeps reminding me, it was he who invited me here, wasn't it? So perhaps it's Robert I should reimburse!'

She would have turned away then, but Mark's heavy hand on her shoulder spun her round. 'And I suppose you and Rob have had some cosy times together at my expense,' he muttered grimly. 'You—you bitch!'

Tobie shook her head again. 'Mark, Robert doesn't even like me. Believe it—it's true. And now, if you'll excuse me—'

'What about me? What about us?'

Mark came after her, stopping her again. 'I won't let you walk out on me.'

'What do you mean?' Tobie was staggered.

'I mean why shouldn't I have what everyone else seems to be offered so freely?' His eyes dropped insinuatively down over her slender body. 'Yes, I've been a fool, I can see that. You obviously respond to rougher treatment.'

His hand groped inexpertly for her bodice, brushing against the rounded curve of her breast, and Tobie was appalled. With a backward step she endeavoured to pull away from him, but her heels were high and she lost her balance, falling heavily against his chest.

'That's better,' he mumbled, his mouth seeking the warm hollows of her neck, while his fingers fumbled at the fastening of her dress. 'You know I could forgive you almost anything, Tobie, when you're near to me like this, but after we're married, I'll kill you if I ever find you with another man!'

'I—am—not—going—to—marry—you!' Tobie got out breathlessly, struggling to free herself. 'Mark, for God's sake, have some sense! Do you want your mother to come out here and find us? What do you think she would say—'

'Mother's gone to bed, I've told you,' Mark retorted, losing patience with the lacing at the front of her chemise dress, and tearing the cords from their holes in his haste. 'Mmm, Tobie, you're beautiful! Let me kiss those delectable breasts—'

The sound of a car engine was like the sweetest music to Tobie's ears, even if it was the noisy chugging of the Mini. It drove into the courtyard below them, the tyres squealing as Cilla applied the brakes, and even Mark was forced to take notice of its significance.

'All right,' he said, as she tore herself away from him. 'I'll let you go for now. But don't lock your door, unless you want me to break it down.'

Tobie stared at him, her face pale, her eyes huge in the moonlight, and then, without a word, she turned away and ran into the house, clutching the remains of her bodice about her, tempted to go straight to his mother and tell her what her precious son had done.

CHAPTER EIGHT

BUT of course she didn't. It would have been too humiliating to tell anyone what had happened, and in her room she paced the floor in real desperation. This was what came of seeking revenge, she thought bitterly. The whole situation had recoiled on her, and now she had nowhere, and no one, to turn to.

She wondered how long it would be before Mark came to find her. She had no doubts that he would come. The alcohol on his breath had convinced her that he had been imbibing rather freely, and his mother's words about Tobie and his brother had been enough to arouse a totally uncharacteristic bravado. She didn't really blame Mark for his behaviour; she blamed his mother. Without her encouragement, he would never have treated Tobie so outrageously. But that didn't alter the fact that he was half drunk and aggressive, and unlikely to think sensibly until the morning.

Standing in the shadows by the open window, she stared unhappily into the darkness. Could she appeal to Robert for assistance? Dared she approach him? And what explanations might he demand that she was ill-prepared to give? Besides, why should she assume he was any different from his brother? He had humiliated her enough in the past. How could she abase herself further, by confessing she was incapable of handling her own life?

Raising a hand to push the heavy weight of her hair back from her hot forehead, she saw the reflection of the moonlight glinting on the yacht, moored down in the harbour. The *Ariadne* was shifting gently on the swell—and suddenly Tobie knew what she was going to do.

Quickly, shedding her torn gown, she rummaged through her wardrobe and brought out a pair of purple denim jeans and a matching silk shirt. Pulling them on, she found her cork-soled sandals and snatched up a cream sweater, in case it was cold later, before leaving her room.

It was nerve-racking threading her way back to the central landing, but she didn't know of any other way out of the villa. It was worse because she didn't exactly know where Mark's rooms were situated, and she could only hope he would wait until the household was asleep before coming after her.

The house seemed quiet enough, but every sound she made was magnified in her ears. She wondered what she would do if Mark stepped out in front of her, and suffered a dozen imaginary shocks when the moonlight played tricks on her. But at last she reached the stairs, and after only a cursory examination of the hall below, she sped down them on winged feet.

She would have to let herself out of the garden room, she decided. She dared not risk making any noise, and the french windows on to the patio were well oiled and silent. Outside, she delayed a moment to close the doors again before running past the pool and down the steps to the courtyard.

It was only as she set off down the road to the harbour that she considered the recklessness of what she was doing. She was a stranger here. She hadn't anticipated what she would do if anyone accosted her, and in the dark shadows between the tall hedges she wondered if Mark's attentions might not be preferable to an assailant's!

She need not have worried. She reached the harbour without mishap, and to her relief there was no one hanging about the boats tied up beside the jetty. The only sounds came from one of the whitewashed cottages, a rhythmic throbbing of calypso music that was curiously soothing, and after a hasty glance around she untied a small rowing boat and dropped silently down into its shallow draught.

It was further to the yacht than she remembered, or perhaps it was simply that her arms were not as strong as Mark's. However, at last she reached the side of the vessel, and securing the rowing boat with its rope she climbed quickly up on to the deck.

She remembered Mark had told her there was a generator on board, but even had she known how to switch it on she wouldn't have done so. The last thing she wanted was to draw attention to herself, and if anyone at the villa saw lights gleaming from the portholes they would probably assume the worst.

Scrambling over a coil of rope, stubbing her

toe on a metal strut, Tobie eventually found her way below. The yacht was very well equipped, and in daylight she had found it a fascinating place, but without any light but moonlight, it was inclined to be eerie. Pools of shadow refused to disperse, no matter how long she stared at them, and the mahogany fitments assumed alien shapes that bore no resemblance to what she remembered.

After stumbling over her third obstacle, Tobie was near to tears, and weariness was weakening her resolve. Was it all worth it? she wondered despairingly, and then chided herself for her weakness. She was here, wasn't she? She was tired, that was all. The simplest and best solution would be to find somewhere to sleep for a few hours. Daylight would waken her, and with a bit of luck she ought to be able to get back to the villa without anyone being any the wiser. Except Mark, perhaps—but he was unlikely to say anything.

Remembering she had seen bunks in the forward cabin, she groped her way to the narrow door and let herself into the sleeping compartment. Yes, she was right. Two single bunks confronted her, and with a sigh of relief she flopped down on to one of them and fell into an exhausted slumber. . .

She awakened to an unfamiliar sound. At first she thought she was back in her own room at Laura's house in Wimbledon, and what she could hear was the steady hum of the traffic on the

Kingston bypass. But as consciousness returned, she realised the sound had vibrations that shook the mattress on which she was lying. *Vibrations*!

All at once, the recollection of the previous night's events returned with horrifying clarity, and as she remembered, so too did she identify the sound that hitherto had eluded her. It was an engine. It was the yacht's engine. Someone was using it—to steer the yacht out of the harbour?

With a gasp she scrambled up on the bunk, peering through the porthole at the receding harbour wall. She didn't need a sextant to calculate that she was too far from land now to swim back to shore, and she chewed anxiously on her fingernail as she wondered who was at the helm.

When the door behind her opened, she swung round guiltily, stifling a cry. Her breathing quickened at the sight of Robert leaning indolently against the frame, and the mocking expression he wore sent her into angry accusation.

'You knew I was here, didn't you?' she exclaimed. 'Where do you think you're taking me?'

Robert moved his shoulders in a dismissing gesture. 'I could say I don't usually make an investigation of the boat before setting sail,' he remarked mildly, and her brow furrowed.

'Don't you need to check your tanks for oil or look in the bilges or something?' she protested, unwilling to acknowledge defeat, and his lips twisted.

'Not in the sleeping berth,' he informed her

shortly. 'How was I to know I'd find a stowaway?'

'I'm not a stowaway.' Tobie was a little uncertain now. 'Didn't you really know I was here?'

Robert hesitated. 'Well, you don't snore,' he admitted dryly; then, as her eyes widened indignantly, he added: 'I could deny it, but I don't. Yes, I knew. As a matter of fact, I was sitting on the patio when you made your escape last night. I was curious, so I followed you.'

Tobie gulped. 'You mean—you spent the night on board, too?'

'I didn't say that.' Robert shifted his weight more comfortably from one leg to the other. 'As soon as I'd assured myself you were safely on board, I went back to the villa. I drove down again about an hour ago.'

Tobie frowned. 'You—drove down—last night?'

Robert shook his head. 'No.'

'But—' Tobie's wave of her hand was expressive.

'I'm not as helpless as my mother would like to believe,' he retorted brusquely. 'I can walk, as you know. Not fast, not particularly gracefully, but I can walk.'

Tobie swung her legs down off the bunk. 'Well, thank you.' She shifted awkwardly. 'Thank you for—well, for caring where I was going.'

Robert straightened. 'No sweat,' he said, glancing behind him. 'I've made some coffee. Do you want some?'

Tobie hesitated. 'I've got to go back, you know.'

'Not yet,' he stated finally, and turning, limped back into the galley.

There was a mirror in the sleeping compartment, and Tobie examined her tumbled hair with some misgivings. She hadn't thought to bring a comb with her, and she had to satisfy herself by using her fingers. It was hardly successful, but it would have to do, and she smoothed the linen cover on the bunk before leaving the cabin.

She shed the chunky cream sweater as she came into the galley. She had been glad of its warmth during the night, but now she could feel the heat of the day penetrating the steel hull. Robert was at the stove, and when she appeared, he handed her a striped beaker of steaming black coffee.

'Mmm, this is delicious,' she murmured, welcoming its reviving strength, and Robert indicated that she should go up on deck to drink it.

It was a beautiful morning. Although it was very early, a glance at her watch had told her it was only a little after seven, the sky was streaked with all the colours of the rainbow. A band of mist obscured the horizon, but the shimmering haze over the water gave the promise of another glorious day. Tobie had never been on a yacht before, and she was slightly apprehensive when Robert cut the engine and began to haul up the sails, but their increase in speed was so exhilarating, she forgot her fears in the sheer delight of the adventure. The *Ariadne* skimmed across the water, the clean, sharp lines of her bow slicing through the waves, leaning slightly to starboard as the crisp breeze filled her canvas.

After securing the ropes—*sheets*. Robert corrected her, when she asked him what he was doing—he came to join her aft, taking charge of the tiller. He explained that depending what degree of sail was presented to the wind, so one governed one's speed and direction, and for a few minutes Tobie forgot their differences in the simple delight of learning something new. Robert had always been able to infuse the most prosaic things with interest, and Tobie listened to what he had to say with evident fascination. She was gazing into his dark face with genuine enthusiasm when she realised he had stopped speaking and was looking at her instead, and she averted her hot face in embarrassment.

'Are you going to tell me why you chose to spend the night on the yacht, rather than sleeping in the comparative luxury of your own bed?' he enquired, his voice curiously hoarse, and she drew a trembling breath before replying.

'I—I was restless,' she lied, avoiding his gaze. 'Go on with what you were telling me about close-hauling. I was interested.'

'I'm interested to know why you felt it necessary to leave the villa,' Robert persisted. 'You needn't have worried, you know. I had no intention of repeating what happened the night before I left for Miami!'

Tobie's head jerked up. Until this moment it had never occurred to her that he might blame

himself for her untimely departure. It was so ludi-
crous, she could only stare at him, and now he
looked away, to gaze broodingly towards an
island far away to their right.

'You're wrong,' she said, making a negative
gesture. 'I mean, my leaving the villa had nothing
to do with you.'

Robert glanced sideways at her. 'No?'

'No.' She shook her head.

'It was only coincidence that sent you running
for cover last night? Are you going to tell me
you've spent the nights I've been away, camping
out on board the *Ariadne*?'

'No.' Tobie sighed heavily, unwilling to admit
why she had left the house. She had enough problems as it was, without adding to them. 'Robert,
honestly, your coming home had nothing to do
with it.'

He raised one canvas-clad foot to rest on the
moulding in front of him, and then turned his
head to study her troubled expression. 'So,'
he said, 'if it wasn't me, it must have been
Mark. What could he possibly have done to
frighten you?'

Tobie moved her head. 'He didn't *frighten* me.'

'Oh, of course.' Robert's mouth hardened.
'How could he? You know one another so well!'

Tobie's lips trembled. 'If that means what I
think it means, I've told you—'

'I know what you told me.' Robert shrugged.
'All right, what did he do?'

Tobie stared at him helplessly for a minute,

then she bent her head. 'He—oh, he was drunk,' she mumbled.

Robert was not appeased. How drunk?'

'How drunk is drunk?' Tobie turned her head away. 'Isn't that an albatross? I've never seen—'

'Tobie!' Robert's hand curved round her jaw, turning her face to his. 'I mean to know. What did Mark say to you? Did he touch you? Was he violent?'

Tobie saw a means of escape. 'He tore my dress,' she conceded, pulling away from him. 'Now are you satisfied?'

'Not entirely,' Robert responded savagely. 'But I can wait.'

Tobie shifted uncomfortably. 'What's that supposed to mean?' And when he didn't answer, she stared about her anxiously. 'Where are we? Oughtn't we to be turning back? He—Mark—and your mother—they'll wonder where I am.'

'No, they won't,' retorted Robert briefly. 'I left word with Henri. I told them I'd taken you for a sail. Does that reassure you?'

Tobie still looked uncertain, but she moved her shoulders in silent acknowledgement. 'I suppose so.'

Robert looked impatient now, and with a determined effort he said: 'Don't look so miserable! You were enjoying it until I started asking awkward questions. Interrogation over! How about a swim?'

'A swim?' Tobie was bemused.

'Yes, a swim.' Robert lifted his arm and pointed to a tiny island just appearing on their right. 'That's a suitable place. We can anchor offshore. The water's not too deep, in case you're anxious.'

Tobie looked unwillingly in the direction he was indicating. 'What is that island?'

'Just one of the cays. I don't suppose it has a name.'

Tobie shook her head. 'I don't have a swimsuit.'

'Nor do I,' retorted Robert dryly. 'Do you really think we need them?'

Tobie's face flamed. 'You can't be serious!'

'Why not?' His dark eyes mocked her. 'I already know what you look like. But if you're prudish about me, don't look.'

Tobie's pulses raced. She had never swum with Robert before. The months she had known him in England, it had been too cold, and although he had planned to take her to Italy, his accident had changed all that. She couldn't call the mishap she had had the morning after she arrived at Soledad swimming, and the prospect of joining him in the water was certainly a temptation.

Without giving him an answer, she went forward to stand in front of the mast, shading her eyes as she surveyed the fast-approaching landfall. It was a thickly-foliaged island, small and apparently deserted, with a shell-like curve of pale sand at the apex of a secluded cove. The water shaded from deep blue to palest turquoise, as the shoreline shelved, and Tobie, feeling the heat of the sun on her shoulders, thought how delightful it would be to submerge herself in its silky depths.

She was unaware Robert had dropped the anchor until he came forward to stand beside her, studying her flushed face with cool interrogation. 'Well?' he prompted. 'What's the verdict? Do I take the plunge on my own, or are you going to be adventurous?'

Tobie sighed. 'Someone might see us,' she protested.

'If that's all that's worrying you, forget it,' he retorted, unbuttoning his denim shirt and taking it off. 'The island's not inhabited, and unless someone's got a powerful telescope trained on us, I doubt they'd know the difference.' He unbuckled his belt. 'But make up your mind. We don't have all day.'

Tobie looked at him, her eyes unwillingly drawn to the solid muscle that made up his chest. He reminded her of a sleek animal, smooth and powerful, and she knew the almost irresistible urge to touch him. She would have liked to have stroked her palms over the olive skin of his shoulders, but when he moved to unzip his pants she abruptly looked away. Even though she remembered his body almost as well as she knew her own, she dared not promote such intimacy, knowing, better than he did, how vulnerable she was.

She heard the splash as he went over the side, and moved to the rail to look down at him. Resting her arms on the steel balustrade, she saw his dark head surface some distance from the boat, and when he saw her watching him he raised an acknowledging hand.

'Come on,' he called. 'The water's quite warm. I promise I won't look.'

Tobie drew back, wrapping her arms about herself. She wanted to join him. Her jeans were warm against her legs, and even the silk shirt was clinging to her back. And it was true, Robert did know what she looked like, better than he knew.

With slightly unsteady fingers she began to unbutton her shirt, drawing into the shelter of the coaming, stripping off her jeans with nervous haste. Then, checking that Robert was still on the landward side of the yacht, she dived into the water at the seaward side, coming up gasping in the sudden enveloping chill.

She had barely recovered from the shock when Robert swam round the prow, his mocking expression mirroring his feelings. But he said nothing, merely gestured that she should follow him, and she swam slowly after him, beginning to enjoy the experience. She had never before realised how constricting clothes could be, and she kicked her legs energetically, luxuriating in the unexpected freedom.

It was warmer closer in to shore, but it was also lighter in the shallower water, and realising this, Tobie remained further out. Nevertheless, she envied Robert's lack of inhibition, watching him from a safe distance, ignoring his calls for her to join him. She caught her breath when he reached a wading depth, but he remained in the water, examining the waving fronds of plant life that grew below the surface, and trying to catch the tiny fish that were present in such quantity.

When he swam back to her she felt absurdly shy, turning away and pretending to be unaware of him. When his hand descended on her head and he deliberately ducked her under the water, she came up gasping furiously, incensed to find him laughing at her some feet away.

'You said you'd stay away from me,' she exclaimed, pushing her wet hair out of her eyes, and his brows quirked in some surprise.

'I didn't—'

'You said you wouldn't touch me, then,' she declared, blinking in the sudden brilliance, but he corrected her with a lazy grimace.

'I said I wouldn't look,' he amended, treading water. 'I said nothing about touching.'

Tobie glared at him. 'You're completely shameless!' she cried, throwing back her head, but he was not perturbed.

'Yes, I am, aren't I?' he agreed, and before she could move away he caught her flailing hand in an iron grip.

'Let go of me!' she fretted, trying to duck him, but once again he was too quick for her.

'With pleasure,' he taunted, his eyes dancing, but he dived underwater before releasing her, taking her with him, and once again she came up spluttering to find he had thwarted her.

'You—you—'

'Swine?' he suggested amicably. 'Monster?' he grinned. 'Bastard?'

'Pig,' declared Tobie succinctly, putting some

distance between them, and then squealed in panic when he reached for her foot.

Yet, in spite of her complaints, she was beginning to enjoy herself. Robert, in this mood, was irresistible, and when he let her get near enough to duck him, too, she paddled away giggling helplessly.

They played for over half an hour, and by the time Robert suggested they went back to the yacht she had almost forgotten her earlier prudishness. Getting out of the water brought it all back to her, however, and she scrambled on to the deck just ahead of Robert, groping wildly for her clothes.

'Wait!' he commanded, right behind her. 'Don't get your clothes wet. I'll get us some towels.'

'All right.'

She half turned her head and then looked back again, and with a derisory sound Robert descended the steps into the cabin. He was back a few seconds later, and pushed a thick orange towel into her hands. With trembling fingers Tobie wrapped it round herself, sarongwise, and then turned automatically to thank him.

Unfortunately, Robert had not expected her to do this, and was in the process of drying himself. Tobie's startled gaze moved over his body to his face, and when she met the smouldering darkness of his eyes, her bones melted.

'For God's sake, Tobie,' he muttered huskily, 'don't look at me like that! Go put your clothes on before I do something we'll both regret.'

Tobie moistened her lips. 'I——I'm sorry,' she murmured, but still she didn't look away, and with a groan of anguish Robert dropped his towel and covered the space between them.

His mouth on hers was only part of the onslaught of feeling his nearness evoked. She was too vulnerable, and as she felt his body close to hers, her defences crumbled. She wanted to be closer to him still, she wanted to feel his body a part of hers, and when his fingers sought the towel that was all that separated them, she guided his hands to the simple knot.

Without that shield, they blended together, skin against skin, softness against hard muscle, fusing together as if they were made for one another. There was no thought of right or wrong, just sensuous, sensual feeling, and the mindless ecstasy of surrender.

His mouth left hers to find the surging peaks of her breasts, tracing their rosy aureoles with his tongue, before enveloping them with his lips. His hands caressed her back, pressing her against him, making her wholly aware of his need of her.

'God, I want you,' he muttered unsteadily, drawing her down on to the deck at their feet and covering her yielding body with his. 'Don't stop me, Tobie. For God's sake, don't stop me now. . .'

She wound her arms around his neck as he spoke, too aroused to deny him anything. 'Love me,' she breathed, her fingers curled in the hair at the nape of his neck, and with a groan of satisfaction he lowered himself on to her.

Tobie's mind spiralled, her lips parting beneath

the hungry pressure of his lips. The hard deck at
her back was forgotten. All she was conscious of
was Robert's hands caressing the curve of her
hips, probing the moist hollows of her thighs,
invading those places only he had known. She
was aching for him to take her, aching for his
possession, and when the consummation came
they melded together in perfect harmony.

'How have I kept my hands off you?' he muttered, as she moved beneath him, and her hands
brought his mouth back to her eager lips.

'Did you want to touch me?' she whispered,
against his ear, as his heart pounded in unison
with hers, and he uttered a rueful groan.

'Did I?' he breathed, tracing the veins at her
temple with his tongue. 'Ah, Tobie, you know
what you do to me, what you've always done to
me. . .'

'Do I?'

She tried to analyse what his words might
mean, but the crescendo was building inside her,
and only his urgent face had any meaning. When
the climax came it was greater than anything she
had ever known, and his anguished: 'Oh, God!'
mingled with her own cry of fulfilment. Her nails
raked his back, but she couldn't help it, and then
they sank together, down through countless
waves of feeling, ebbing and flowing around them
in slowly-decreasing intensity. Tobie felt totally
submerged, totally complete, for the first time
since she and Robert were so violently separated.

Some minutes later Robert, whose face had
been buried in the hollow of her neck, lifted his

head and let tantalising fingers brush the damp hair back from her forehead.

'Thank you,' he said huskily, and when her brows drew uncomprehendingly together, a faint smile touched his lips. 'I'd not put it to the test,' he explained, his fingertips finding her lips. 'I could have been impotent, like you said.'

Tobie gazed up at him. 'I didn't say that,' she protested. 'And—and in any case, what about Cilla?'

'What about Cilla?' He frowned.

Tobie was nervous with him, even now. 'I thought—I mean, you and she—'

'Oh, I see.' Robert's lips twisted. 'Well, no. Cilla and I never have.'

Tobie hesitated. 'And—and was it—good?'

'Good?' Much to her regret, he drew away from her then, sitting up and drawing up one leg to rest his chin on his knee. 'It was better than good, as I'm sure you know.'

Tobie eased herself up on her elbows. 'Why— why did you say—I would know what I did to you?' Her lips quivered. 'What did you mean by that?'

Robert turned his head then and looked at her. 'What did you think I meant?'

Tobie's mouth felt dry. 'I asked you.'

Robert studied her anxious expression for a few moments, and then, without answering her, he got to his feet. 'I need to cool off,' he said, his tone curiously flat. 'You can shower down below, if you want to. I'll use nature's way.'

She wanted to delay him, to persist with her

questioning until she knew, once and for all, whether he really did know who she was. But she couldn't. When she opened her mouth to speak, the words wouldn't come, and he dived into the water again without her saying anything.

CHAPTER NINE

ROBERT was dressed by the time she emerged from the cabin, already hauling up the anchor and making ready to sail. His acknowledgement of her reappearance was brief and expressionless, and Tobie, seating herself in the stern, felt chilled and uncertain. It seemed hardly credible that less than an hour before he had been trembling in her arms. Now he seemed cool and remote, more remote than early this morning, when he first found her in the cabin.

Tobie shook her head. What had gone wrong? What had she said to change his mood from one of lazy indulgence to cold, detached indifference? Why was he treating her this way? Now that he had had his way with her, did he despise her for giving in to him?

He was hauling up the sail, and on impulse she went to join him, offering her assistance in dragging up the canvas.

'I can manage,' he replied, refusing her help abruptly. 'If you want to do something useful, go and make some more coffee. I could certainly use a cup.'

Tobie hesitated, and then with a helpless shrug she complied, swinging down the steps into the galley, and blinking back the stupid tears as she searched for the jar of grains. Why had she imagined their making love would change anything? she demanded of herself tremulously. She was a woman, not a silly schoolgirl, and Robert had certainly known she was no virgin. What had she expected? Some soulful declaration from him, when that was not, and had never been, his way?

She boiled the kettle and made the instant coffee, carrying it up the steps with some difficulty. However, she managed, offering the tray to Robert first before taking a beaker for herself.

Robert was at the helm, sprawled beside the tiller, his brooding expression no encouragement to conversation. But Tobie refused to allow him to see how he was hurting her by adopting this attitude, and seating herself beside him she gave him a bright smile.

'It's only eleven o'clock,' she remarked, ignoring his dark malevolence. 'We should be back at Emerald Cay before twelve.'

Robert inclined his head in silent acquiescence, but she was determined not to be thwarted by his evident self-absorption. 'Just imagine,' she proceeded, desperately trying to hide the tremor in her voice, 'this time tomorrow we'll probably be on our way back to England.'

That, at least, evoked some reaction. 'Tomorrow?' Robert repeated harshly. 'You're leaving tomorrow?'

'Yes.' Tobie couldn't sustain the piercing penetration of his stare, and assumed an interest in the coffee in her cup. 'Didn't you know? Mark has to be back in London the day after.'

'And of course you're going with him,'

he averred savagely. 'When are you getting married?'

Tobie caught her breath. 'You—ask me that?'

Robert said a word she wouldn't like to repeat. 'Why not? That's why you came here, isn't it? Just because—well, just because I find you very beddable, it doesn't mean anything, does it? You knew what you were doing when you came.'

Tobie trembled. 'What's that supposed to mean?'

'You *know*!' Robert's lips curled contemptuously. 'Oh, come on! Let's stop kidding ourselves, shall we? We both know why you came here. To get even with me. Oh, yes—' this, as her eyes widened in sudden comprehension, 'I remember you, Tobie. I remember everything. I may have forgotten for a few days. I can't honestly recall much of what happened immediately after the crash, but by the end of the first week I was pretty sure of how it happened.'

Tobie couldn't say anything. She just put down her coffee and stared at him, and with an impatient grimace, he went on: 'Okay, so now you know. Does that make us even? I would have told you sooner, but I wanted to see how far you would go.'

That hurt. Unable to prevent herself, she slapped him then, slapped him and punched him, and fought him like the wildcat she felt at this cruel betrayal.

'You—you swine!' she choked, when he had both her hands imprisoned in one of his, successfully preventing any further liberties on her part. 'Oh, I—I hate you!'

'Why?' He arched his brows interrogatively. 'What did I do? Only set the record straight, as I've been expecting you to do ever since you came here!'

Tobie gasped. 'But you knew—you knew your mother would tell me you'd lost your memory. She believes it, too, or so she says.'

Robert shrugged. 'Sometimes I wonder. Perhaps it suits her to believe it. As it suited you.'

'What do you mean?'

'Oh, come on. . .' He gave her an old-fashioned look. 'You knew if I suspected who you were, things might get very—complicated.'

'But you did know—'

'You didn't know that.'

Tobie made a helpless gesture. 'You *hate* me that much?'

'I don't hate you at all.' Robert glared at her in a way that contradicted his statement. 'I wanted to. My God, I wanted to. But you knew you had only to snap your fingers and I'd come running!'

Tobie gulped. 'How can you say that?'

'Why do you think I let them go on thinking I couldn't remember what had happened?' he snarled violently. 'Do you think I wanted to be reminded of what you'd done?'

'What I'd done?' Tobie faltered. 'Don't you mean—what you'd done?'

'What I'd done? What had I done?' he demanded harshly. 'Only given you everything I had to give! Been driven half out of my mind every time some other man spoke with you, smiled at you, *touched* you!' His mouth tightened. 'Oh, yes, Tobie, you chose your weapons well. My own brother was the ideal target.'

Tobie endeavoured to free herself, but when she couldn't, she was forced to plead with him. 'It wasn't like that,' she exclaimed. 'I didn't know who Mark was when I first got to know him.'

'No?'

'No. How could I? You'd never mentioned him. How was I supposed to find out?'

'And when you did? Find out, I mean. How did you feel then?'

How had she felt? Tobie licked her lips. 'I don't remember.' But she did! She remembered the sensation of disbelief, the sudden pain like a knife in her stomach, the trembling awareness of what was within her grasp.

'I don't believe you,' Robert said now, releasing her so abruptly she almost fell off the seat. 'You must have felt something. Something so intense, you decided to take your revenge in the savagest way possible.'

'No!' Tobie shook her head. 'It wasn't like that.'

'What was it like, then?'

'I—I—I couldn't believe it at first.'

'That I do believe.'

'Robert, please. Listen to me.' She pressed her palms to the sides of her neck. 'It isn't like you think. I didn't come here to—to punish you—'

'To punish yourself, perhaps?'

'Why should I want to do that?'

Robert raked back his hair with hands that were not steady. 'You know why. Why did you do it, Tobie? Why didn't you tell me? Why couldn't you have waited? Or was the state I was in too much for you to stand?'

The—state you were in?' Tobie was confused. 'What are you talking about?'

'Me! The mess I looked after the crash. You couldn't even bear to come and see me—Mother told me. I had no visitors. Phone calls, of course, and the press, who were kept away. But no visitors.'

'That's not true!' Tobie caught his arm. 'I did come.'

Robert's brows descended. 'You came to see me? Then why didn't my mother—'

'No, no—I came to the hospital, but I didn't see you.' Tobie was getting desperate. 'They—they wouldn't let me. I—I was told you'd expressly forbidden me to be admitted.'

'Oh, come on.' Robert gazed at her disbelievingly. 'I was in no state to forbid anything.'

'I didn't know that. I didn't even know you'd been badly hurt until I came here. You kept it out of the papers—you just said so.'

'Even so. . .' Robert shook his head, 'I couldn't have issued instructions like that. I was unconscious half the time.'

'Perhaps it was your mother,' Tobie voiced her own suspicions. 'Oh, God, it must have been her—'

'No.' Robert's jaw was hard. 'She wouldn't do that.'

'Why not?'

'Why not?' Robert made a helpless gesture. 'Well—because there was no point. . .'

Tobie hunched her shoulders. 'Perhaps there was.' She sighed. 'Someone stopped me from seeing you.'

Robert expelled his breath heavily. 'All right. So why didn't you come back? If I meant that much to you, why didn't you try again?'

Tobie bent her head. 'I couldn't.'

'Oh, of course.' Robert's mouth hardened again. 'You were in the hospital, too, weren't you? How long was that? Two days? Three? How long did it take to buy your freedom?'

Tobie couldn't answer him. It was all too much. Much too much. He was never going to understand, and she simply hadn't the strength to go on fighting with him. Besides, how could she tell him what had happened to her now? How would he feel about it? Dared she risk that last shred of self-respect by confessing everything? She knew she couldn't, so she said nothing.

'Well,' he remarked at last, when it became obvious she was not going to answer him. 'Perhaps you could explain why you didn't tell me about the baby? Didn't I have a right to know? It was my child, wasn't it?'

Tobie's breath escaped on a sob. 'You know it was.'

'Very well.' His face was grim. 'Why didn't you explain that that was the reason you wanted us to get married?'

Tobie's lips parted. 'You—you really think I

could have done that? Asked you to marry me because I was pregnant?'

'It has been done,' he retorted dryly.

'Not by me.'

'Why not?'

Tobie turned her back on him, gripping the side of the boat so tightly it dug painfully into her palms. 'I don't want to talk about it any more,' she said, through stiff lips. 'I don't ever want to talk to you again.'

Robert's hand on her shoulder forced her round to look at him. 'We are going to talk again, Tobie,' he told her, his eyes offering no compromise. 'If not now, then later, when I've got to the bottom of this.'

'No—'

'Yes.' His determination was frightening. 'And you needn't bother to pack your bags. You're not leaving here tomorrow. I want you where I can find you. God knows, it took long enough for us to get together. I'm not letting you go again, not yet. Not until *I'm* satisfied.'

Tobie tore herself away from him, putting the width of the deck between them. 'You can't make me stay,' she retorted, panic giving her an unnatural bravado, and his eyes glittered dangerously.

'Try and leave,' he challenged her coldly, and as she struggled for a response, she had to acknowledge that here on Emerald Cay he held all the cards.

He didn't say anything after that, and neither did she, huddled forward by the mast, a prey to her own neuroses. She wondered if it was possible to have a relapse, even after all this time, and shook at the memory of those endless days at Riderbeck. It was incredible that one man could have done that to her, and she closed her eyes against the mental images that persisted in tormenting her. She had thought he had changed, but he hadn't, and remembering how eagerly she had surrendered to him filled her with a hopeless sense of failure. Laura was right: she should not have come here, and given the chance, she would put as many miles between her and Robert as was humanly possible.

The little quayside on Emerald Cay was buzzing with activity. Robert lowered the sails and used the engine to steer the yacht between the horns of the reef, then dropped anchor in the harbour. Tobie, rousing herself with reluctance, refused the offer of his hand to climb down into the dinghy, and although she twisted her ankle as she made a rather undignified descent into the tiny craft, she said nothing. However, as Robert rowed them back to the shore, her attention was distracted by the men unloading a cargo freighter that had docked in their absence. The swinging crates containing meat and dried goods, fruit and vegetables, and other domestic essentials reminded her painfully of how much she was going to miss the warmth and colour of the island. She had known a curious kind of happiness here, she realised, being near Robert again. And, if that precarious state of mind had been shattered now, she could still regret its passing. She looked at Robert then, wondering if he shared any shred of compassion, and then realised he wasn't even aware of her at that moment. His attention was fixed on the quay, and when she turned to look where he was looking she saw Henri, standing shading his eyes, evidently watching for them.

Tobie knew an immediate sense of disquiet, and her jumbled thoughts sought for some explanation for his waiting presence. Had something happened? Was Robert's mother ill? Or had Mark sent Henri on some mission of his?

She looked back at Robert, and saw his lean face, dark now with fatigue. It had been an exhausting morning for him, she realised, unable to prevent her errant pulses from leaping at the memory of his lovemaking. For that was what it had been. Whatever had gone before and whatever came after, Robert had made love to her, and that was something she would remember.

Meeting his eyes suddenly, she averted her own, afraid to let him read what she had been thinking. He had taken enough from her as it was. He should not have the satisfaction of knowing that she still loved him, even if she didn't like him very much.

Henri stretched out to catch the rope that Robert threw to him as they neared the quay. He secured the dinghy as his master shipped the oars, then reached down to help him on to the jetty, his black face creased with excitement.

'I been looking for you, sir,' he exclaimed, anxiously waiting while Robert gave Tobie his hand, which this time she accepted. 'It's Mr Jennings, sir—Missy Cilla's father. He been taken ill, sir, and Missy Cilla taking it badly.'

Robert released Tobie as soon as she had gained her balance, his concern apparent as he gripped Henri's arm. 'Harvey?' he exclaimed disbelievingly, shaking his head. 'Harvey's sick? What is it? What's wrong with him? Does anyone know?'

'Mr Mark, sir, he say it a stroke,' Henri explained, with some pride in remembering the word. 'It must have happened during the night. Missy Cilla find him this morning—on the floor. Unconscious!'

Even without Henri's sense of the dramatic, it was shocking news, and Robert glanced rather absently at Tobie as he tried to marshal his thoughts. 'I'd better get over there,' he muttered, thinking rapidly. 'You take Miss Kennedy back to the villa, Henri, and I'll take the jeep over to the Jennings' place.'

'Yes, sir.'

Henri was eager to comply, but Tobie felt curiously loath to let Robert go. 'When will you—I mean, is there anything I can do?' she finished lamely, as his gaze was turned upon her, but Robert was in no mood to be tactful.

'Go back to the villa,' he directed tersely, as Henri turned politely away. 'Do as I told you. And I'll see you later.'

Tobie's lips trembled. 'I'm not a little girl, Robert,' she retorted, in a scarcely audible undertone, and his eyes darkened ominously.

'No, you're not,' he agreed, gripping her neck with barely-suppressed violence. 'And believe me, this is the last thing I could have wished to happen—for several reasons. But I don't have time to argue with you now. I just want your word that you'll do as I say, and not create any more problems than I have already.'

'*You* have problems!' she taunted, knowing she was behaving badly, but somehow sensing this might be her last chance. 'You don't know the meaning of the word!' and dragging herself away from him, she ran after Henri. The last image she had was of Robert still standing there, staring after her, his face contorted with an emotion she had never seen before.

The villa seemed strangely deserted when she returned. There was no one about, and although breakfast had been laid on the glass-topped table on the patio, no one appeared to have touched the jug of iced orange juice, or sampled the now lukewarm rolls under their perspex shield. Of course, Mark was at the Jennings' house, lending his professional assistance, and with Robert absent too, Tobie felt curiously vulnerable.

As her hair was still damp from her swim, she went to dry it, using the hand-drier Mrs Newman had offered that first morning she was at Soledad. She was glad of the distraction. She wished there was something useful she could do. But as Cilla was already on hand to offer her help, she could only wait in helpless anticipation.

She started, when the door to the downstairs bathroom opened behind her, and her doubts of minutes before crystallised at Mrs Newman's appearance. Mark's mother was obviously not surprised to find her, and Tobie guessed that that had been her intention.

'So you're back,' she remarked, with unnecessary emphasis. 'I thought it must be you. I imagine Robert's gone tearing over to the Jennings', hasn't he?'

Tobie turned off the drier. 'Henri told him what had happened,' she admitted. 'Naturally he went to see if he could help.'

'Naturally.' Mrs Newman's lips twisted. 'Did you enjoy your sail?'

Tobie tried to remain casual. 'Very much,' she averred. 'I've never done any sailing before.'

'Haven't you?' The older woman raised her eyebrows. 'No, I don't suppose you have. Girls from your background seldom get the opportunity.'

It was said mildly enough, but it was an insult nevertheless, and Tobie had to steel herself not to rise to the bait. 'No, I don't suppose we do,' she responded, deliberately misunderstanding her. 'The weather in England is so unpredictable, and one rarely finds a suitable weekend.'

It was not what Mrs Newman had meant, and they both knew it. But short of forcing the issue, there was nothing she could say. Putting the drier aside, Tobie reached for the brush and began to stroke its bristles through her hair. She thought, rather shakily, that she had won that particular point, and when, after a moment's hesitation, Mrs Newman left her she breathed a sigh of relief.

But it was not over. Mrs Newman was waiting

in the hall when Tobie emerged from the bathroom, and she suggested they had coffee together
on the patio.

'I've asked Monique to fetch us a fresh pot,'
she said, urging the girl outside, and Tobie was
hard pressed to find an excuse.

'Really,' she murmured, 'I don't want anything
right now, thank you. I—er—I'm a little tired. I
thought I might lie down for a while.'

'Surely you won't leave me to take refreshment
alone?' Mrs Newman's expression was challeng-
ing now. 'After all, you are a guest in my house.
I've asked very little of you so far.'

Tobie could have said that it was Robert's
house, and that Mrs Newman herself had made
it plain that she had not wanted her here, but she
didn't. Instead she allowed herself to be coaxed
into a chair in the shade of the awning, and
accepted the cup of coffee that Monique's
reappearance afforded.

'We'll have lunch in half an hour,' Mrs
Newman ordered as the black maid departed. 'I
don't suppose my sons will join us. I imagine
they'll remain with Miss Cilla until after the helicopter has arrived.

'The helicopter?' exclaimed Tobie involuntarily, as Monique nodded and left them. 'Is Mr
Jennings being taken to hospital?'

The older woman regarded her coldly for a
moment, then inclined her head. 'At Mark's
suggestion, yes, he is,' she replied, raising her
cup to her lips and sipping the strong black liquid.
'It's necessary that Harvey should receive the

most efficient treatment possible, and without the appropriate equipment Mark's contribution is limited.'

'Of course.' Tobie was concerned. 'How ill is he? Can Mark make a diagnosis?'

'I really don't see of what possible interest it can be to you,' retorted Mrs Newman bleakly. 'The Jennings are hardly friends of yours, merely acquaintances, and the state of Harvey's health is our affair, not yours.'

Tobie caught her breath at the hostility in Mrs Newman's voice. She could see no reason why the older woman should feel it necessary to treat her in this way, and she could only assume that until now Mark's presence had provided a buttress.

Choosing her words carefully, she said: 'I'd be concerned about anybody in the same situation. And I really don't see why you invited me to join you, Mrs Newman, if my company arouses such antagonism.'

It was bravely said, and for a moment the older woman was taken aback. But not for long. 'I asked you to join me because I wanted to talk to you,' she declared, setting down her cup. 'I wanted to ask you what your intentions are concerning my sons.'

'Your sons?' Tobie was flabbergasted now. 'You make it sound as if I had designs on both of them!'

'I think you have had, in your time,' retorted Mrs Newman smoothly. 'We both know you knew Robert before his accident, and as soon as

you got to know who Mark was, you got your
claws into him, too.'

'That's not true!'

'It is true.' Mrs Newman's mouth compressed.
'I know. I was there the day you came to the
hospital, begging to see Robert. I knew what you
were the first time I laid eyes on you!'

Tobie uttered a shocked cry. 'You mean—it
was you—'

'—who turned you away? Yes. I'm not
ashamed to admit it. You were no good for
Robert, I could see that. And in the event, you've
proved me right.'

'No—'

'Yes.' The older woman was implacable in her
hatred. 'As soon as I heard your name I had my
suspicions, and when I saw you. . .'

Tobie licked her dry lips. 'So why did you
let me come here? It's obvious you have some
influence with Mark. Why didn't you forbid it?'

'How could I?' Mrs Newman was grim.
'Robert insisted he wanted to meet you. This is
his island, *his* house. How could I prevent you
coming without arousing suspicions?'

'I see.' Tobie touched her temple with the tips
of her fingers. 'So it was Robert who brought me
here. . .'

'Not for the reasons you would like to
imagine,' retorted his mother coldly. 'You forget,
Robert doesn't know you. He was curious, that's
all. Now his curiosity has been satisfied. My
gamble has paid off.'

'Your—gamble?'

'Of course. It was a gamble allowing you to come here. His memory could have been jolted.' Her face twisted into the semblance of a smile, but it was not a pleasant expression. 'Instead, I got what I wanted—and so will Mark.'

'What—you wanted?' Tobie was bewildered.

'Yes. Mark told me this morning. You and he—it's all over. I knew it would be, once he found out what you were.'

'What I was?'

'A tramp, Miss Kennedy,' said the older woman succinctly. 'Someone without morals or self-respect. Someone who'll sleep with any man who shows an interest—'

Tobie's chair overturned as she got to her feet. 'You're lying!' she choked, instilled with a feeling of loathing so great it almost overwhelmed her powers of speech. 'I've never slept with any man but Robert, and you know it!'

'Do I?' Mrs Newman looked up at her without compassion. 'I suppose you're going to tell me it was Robert's child you were expecting, that day you came to the hospital.'

Tobie couldn't believe this. 'I—of course it was Robert's child,' she got out with difficulty. Then, as comprehension dawned: 'You *knew*?'

'I'm a woman,' stated Mrs Newman chillingly. 'I recognised the symptoms. There's a certain look a woman has when—'

'But you didn't see me!'

'Oh, yes, I saw you. You, however, did not see me.'

Tobie could feel herself beginning to shake,

and a sense of panic gripped her. She couldn't break down here, she thought wildly, not in front of this woman.

'I didn't need to tell Mark, naturally,' Mrs Newman continued. 'It was enough for him to know that you and Robert—'

'*No!*'

The denial was torn from her, and Tobie felt the tears she had been fighting for so long beginning to have their way with her. She couldn't stop them. They poured down her cheeks, running off the tip of her nose, invading the parted softness of her lips.

'Tears won't arouse my sympathy,' the older woman went on relentlessly. 'I'm so relieved that Mark has seen through you. I knew he would. He's not like Robert. Robert was always wilful— reckless! Blaming me for his father's weakness.' Her lips curled. 'Mark is my son, my *real* son. He's the one I care about. You don't imagine I've enjoyed humbling myself before Robert, do you? Living here with him, making myself indispensable. But Mark needs money to continue with his career, and I'd do anything to ensure his future.'

Tobie scraped her palms across her cheeks. 'Mark's future is assured,' she exclaimed. 'He's a doctor.'

'He's a junior houseman at an inferior hospital,' retorted Mrs Newman scathingly. 'Mark has ambition. He wants to specialise. If he could open his own clinic—either here, or in London—'

Tobie sniffed. 'Why are you telling me all

this? Aren't you afraid I'll tell Robert?'

'Who would believe you?' Mrs Newman's smile was smug, an unpleasant rictus. 'Not Robert. He doesn't remember you. And would you expose yourself—expose how you turned away in horror when you found he might be paralysed?'

'I didn't!'

'Try telling him that. Robert's very sensitive about such things. And he might just believe the child was his!'

Tobie tried to think. She was tempted to tell this woman that Robert already knew who she was, had already exposed her naïve attempt to deceive him. But to do so meant betraying the things Robert had told her, and after what she had learned just now she could not do that.

'I suggest we understand' one another,' Mrs Newman was saying now, returning to her seat again. 'I wanted to make my position clear, and I've done so. Naturally you won't discuss any of this with Mark. You'll return with him to London tomorrow, and that will be the end of it.'

Tobie's features felt frozen. 'You think you hold all the cards, don't you?' she choked.

'I believe I do,' the older woman remarked smoothly, as the droning vibration of rotor blades attracted their eyes upward. 'Ah, good, the helicopter has arrived. If you'll excuse me, I must go and see about lunch.'

She was so matter-of-fact, apparently caring as little about Harvey Jennings' attack as she did about everything else—except Mark. Left to herself, Tobie righted her chair, but did not sit down upon it. She felt exhausted, both physically and emotionally, and her head was aching quite abominably. What a situation! she thought, her palms curving over the fan-shaped arc at the back of her chair. What could she do? And what was more to the point, what *should* she do?

Could she go to Robert and expose his mother? It would be her word against Tobie's, and why should she expect him to believe her? He hadn't done so far, and there was still a barrier between them. Could she risk everything on one final desperate throw?

Scuffing her feet, she went into the villa and climbed the stairs to her room. It was unnaturally tidy, and it wasn't until she began to look through the drawers that she realised someone had already been through them. They were empty. Her clothes had gone. And when she saw the suitcases sitting neatly on the ottoman she knew why. Her belongings had been packed for her. Mrs Newman was taking no chances that she should not be ready to leave in the morning. Only one evening dress had been left hanging in the wardrobe, obviously for this evening, but everything else, even her swimsuits, had been systematically stowed away.

It was what she had needed. Mrs Newman might never know it, but she had just pushed Tobie too far. The sight of those expertly-filled suitcases was enough to bring her to her senses. Until then she had been wavering, torn by the knowledge of what Robert had accused her, weakened by the need to protect him, and reluctant to submit to his demands. Now her doubts evaporated. She *would* tell Robert. She would tell him everything, and risk whatever came after. What had she got to lose, after all, except perhaps those remnants of self-respect she had saved on the yacht, and they would be cold comfort in the years to come. Better to risk everything and be completely honest with him, than run away to live her life, always wondering what might have been. To do that would not only cheat Robert but herself.

CHAPTER TEN

SHE even managed to eat some lunch, although by late afternoon her confidence was waning. The hours had passed slowly, and although she had waited patiently, neither Robert nor Mark had appeared.

It was Monique who eventually told her. 'Mr Robert and Mr Mark—they gone with Mr Jennings,' she explained, when Tobie ventured into the kitchen, ostensibly in search of tea. 'Missy Cilla, she too upset to go alone, and Mr Mark, he want to talk with the doctor at the hospital.'

'I see.' Tobie's spirits plummeted. 'I wonder what time they'll get back.'

'Don't know, missy. You like something to eat?'

'Oh, no. No.' Tobie shook her head almost absently, absorbed with her thoughts. 'Tea will be fine, Monique. I—I'll be on the patio.'

'Yes'm.' Monique smiled, and leaving her, Tobie trudged across the hall and out on to the terrace.

It was a humid afternoon, the sky tinged a curious shade of ochre. At home, she would have surmised that they were in for a thunderstorm, and she wondered if that was what the humidity portended. If it was, it was unlikely that Robert and Mark would get back from Castries that evening. Until then she had not considered what she would do if Robert didn't get back, but now frustration crystallised like a hard ball inside her. She might not even see him in the morning. She and Mark were planning to leave before lunch. Their plane was due to leave in the late afternoon. What chance would she have of talking to Robert, if Mark was breathing down her neck? Robert's demand that she should stay, she discounted. Cilla's needs evidently came first, and that should convince her of something.

Mrs Newman appeared as she was drinking her second cup of tea, and Tobie looked up at her half apprehensively. But for once the other woman was not concerned with their relationship, scanning the sky anxiously, confirming Tobie's suspicions.

'There's been a storm warning on the radio,' she admitted unwillingly, linking and unlinking her fingers. 'I wonder what time Mark will get back.'

Tobie decided there was nothing to be gained by remaining silent. 'Will they come back tonight, if the weather's bad?' she asked, shrugging her slim shoulders, and Mrs Newman made a sound of impatience.

'Of course Mark will come back,' she exclaimed. 'He wouldn't stay away, not when it's his last night.' She compressed her thin lips. 'Robert—well, Robert is a law unto himself. If Cilla needs him, I imagine he'll insist on staying with her.'

Tobie digested this piece of information without comment. It was what she had expected, after all, and she resigned herself to the conclusion that fate had decreed it so.

The breeze blowing up from the harbour was strengthening, rippling the waters of the pool, bending the sprays of blossom that twined over the *cabañas*. Clouds were scurrying hurriedly across the sky, and the first drops of rain sprinkled the terrace. The radio warning had not been ill timed. They were in for a downpour, and whether the helicopter would return this evening was becoming very doubtful.

'Mark couldn't stay away—he *wouldn't*!' Mrs Newman insisted, gazing anxiously towards the heavens, and Tobie was moved to reassure her.

'I don't suppose he wants to,' she said, lifting her shoulders helplessly. 'But you wouldn't want him to risk his life, or that of the pilot's, by flying back in bad weather, would you?'

'He will come back,' exclaimed Mrs Newman, pulling out her handkerchief and twisting it tortuously. 'He *must*! He knows how I hate storms!'

'Oh, I see.' Tobie grimaced. This was something she had not considered. Mrs Newman seemed so strong, so invincible. It hardly seemed possible that a little thing like a thunderstorm should distress her. 'Well, don't worry. I'm here, and storms don't frighten me.'

Mrs Newman gave her a disdainful look. 'Mark will be here,' she affirmed tightly, and turning, walked back into the house.

The sky was getting much darker now, and

Tobie decided she might as well go indoors too. Mrs Newman had switched on the hall lights, and the chandelier cast its illumination in a thousand prisms. It was strange, having the lights on in the afternoon, another curious facet to this curiously unreal day.

In her room, she sat by the window, watching the clouds deepening. It would be quite a change to see the rain, she thought. So many days of fine weather could become monotonous. The plants would welcome a watering. Henri did his best, but it was never enough. A change of scene was what they all needed, she decided wearily, and thought, with sudden nostalgia, of her home in Wimbledon. She wondered what Laura would say if she told her everything that had happened. Laura was notoriously partisan; she would never accept that Robert had any justification for his beliefs. In her eyes, everything was either black or white, and so far as she was concerned, Robert was to blame—for everything.

It was almost dark when she heard the sound of the helicopter. She couldn't believe that was what it was at first. She thought perhaps it was the low rumble of distant thunder, but as the sound increased she realised it was an aircraft.

Immediately her nerves tightened. Had Robert come back? Was she, after all, to be given the chance to speak with him? And why, if that were so, did she suddenly feel so inadequate?

Realising she could not go down in the shirt and jeans she had worn all day, she stripped off her clothes and took a shower, wearing a cap to protect her hair. Then, suitably lipsticked and mascaraed, she put on the white chiffon evening gown Mrs Newman had left unpacked and descended the stairs on anxious feet.

A man was standing in the drawing room, and she halted in the doorway uncertainly. He was tall and dark, yet curiously bulky, and as he turned, she realised this must be the helicopter pilot. He was wearing a navy blue uniform, and as her eyes adjusted themselves to the lamplight she saw the peaked cap lying on the nearby table. Looking into his swarthy Latin-type features, she wondered how she could have mistaken him for Robert, and then realised she was so emotionally tense, any dark man could confuse her.

'Hi,' he said, and his accent was unmistakably American. 'I'm George Capra. Pleased to meet you.'

Tobie allowed her hand to be enveloped in his huge paw, forcing a smile of welcome. 'How do you do, Mr Capra,' she responded politely. 'So you made it here after all.'

'Hell, yes.' The pilot nodded vigorously towards the streaming windows. 'This here is just the tail-end of the storm, Miss—er—'

'Kennedy,' Tobie supplied briefly, and he went on:

'Well, Miss Kennedy, we have been mighty lucky, yes, indeed. Seems like we had a hurricane licking its way west of here, but all we got was the backlash.'

'A hurricane!' Tobie was appalled.

'You never seen a hurricane, Miss Kennedy?'

'No, I haven't.' Tobie caught her lower lip between her teeth. 'Was anyone hurt?'

George Capra shrugged his bulky shoulders. 'No one's been killed, if that's what you mean. Luckily she blew herself out off the coast of Cuba.'

Tobie shook her head. 'And yet you flew back here?'

'Mr Newman, he seemed pretty anxious about you ladies. I said I'd bring him back if he offered me a bed for the night.'

'It was the least I could do,' said Mark, from the doorway, and Tobie turned to face him. It was the first time she had seen him since their unfortunate confrontation of the night before, but although her skin prickled, it was Mark who turned red. 'Hello, Tobie,' he greeted her rather stiffly, running a finger round the inside of his collar, as if it was too tight for him. 'Have you had a good day?'

Tobie thought the question ill timed, but she made a casual response. 'It's been—oppressive,' she replied, wondering if he was aware of the ambiguity. 'How is Mr Jennings? Did he recover consciousness? Has Cilla come back with you?'

'Harvey's going to be all right,' Mark said shortly. 'It was a stroke, but he'll get over it. He may sustain some paralysis, who can tell at this stage, but it's my opinion that he'll make a complete recovery.'

Tobie was disturbed by his indifference. She knew he didn't like Harvey, but she was dismayed by his attitude. 'And Cilla?' she persisted, glancing awkwardly at George Capra. 'Has she gone home?'

'Cilla didn't come back with us,' stated Mark, walking across to the tray of drinks and uncorking the Scotch. 'On the rocks?' he suggested, waving the bottle at the pilot, and Capra nodded in some embarrassment. 'She wanted to stay at the hospital, so they've provided a room for her.'

'I see.' Tobie digested this while Mark poured the drinks, and shook her head when he offered her the same.

'Rob stayed at the hospital, too,' he added, raising his glass to his lips. 'I guess he thinks Cilla needs him.' He shook his head. 'He told me to tell you goodbye.'

Tobie turned away so that he should not see how his words had affected her. She had absorbed the news that Robert had not returned with grim fortitude, still clinging to the faint hope that he might return in the morning before they were due to leave. Mark's careless statement had negated that hope, leaving her with a feeling of complete devastation.

'Dinner won't be long, George,' Mark was saying now, and Tobie was glad of the bluff pilot's presence. She did not think she could have exchanged polite conversation right at that moment, and indeed, she faced the prospect of joining them for dinner with a sense of desperation. She longed for the evening to be over, to bring the morning that much sooner, and she knew she would not relax until she was on board the plane to London.

Dinner was served half an hour later, with Mrs Newman presiding over the table. She obviously enjoyed the unexpected privilege, and she and the American did most of the talking. Tobie felt Mark's eyes on her from time to time, and wondered what he was thinking. Had his mother discussed with him the conversation she had had with Tobie that morning? No, of course not. That was not for publication. Mrs Newman would no doubt content herself by consolidating the position she already held, and after Tobie's behaviour the night before, Mark probably considered he was the injured party. She wondered if he had gone to her room, and if he had, what he had thought when he found it empty. Meeting his eyes across the flickering candle flame, she thought she saw a trace of anxiety in their depths, and guessed he was afraid she might betray him to his mother. He need not have worried, she thought dryly. Nothing she said would convince Mrs Newman he was anything other than a misunderstood boy, and remembering the good times they had had together, she half wished she could reassure him. In spite of what had happened, he was not entirely to blame for his misapprehension, and she condemned his mother for fostering his resentment. Even so, she was sensible enough to realise that Mark was as unlikely to be critical of his mother as she was of him, and in either case, Tobie was simply banging her head against a brick wall.

Nevertheless, she sensed a certain cautiousness in his attitude towards her, and never once did he refer to the previous evening's events. On the contrary, if anything he avoided her attention, and it was left to George Capra to entertain the female members of the party.

It was towards the end of the evening that Mark dropped his bombshell. Under cover of the anecdote the American was relating with some hilarity to his mother, he told an astounded Tobie that he would not be returning with her to London.

'I sent a telegram from Castries this afternoon,' he said, speaking in an undertone. 'I don't think it would be fair to leave, in the circumstances, and Mother agrees with me.'

She would, thought Tobie dryly, and then shook her head. 'Aren't you afraid the hospital board may dismiss you? They're bound to be suspicious when you've been on holiday for two weeks.'

'I don't care if they do,' replied Mark indifferently. 'I'm bored with working in London. I'd welcome a change of scene.'

Tobie could think of nothing to say. She guessed his mother was at the bottom of this. Perhaps Mrs Newman suspected that Mark might have second thoughts about her once they were back in England. After all, he was a different person away from his mother's influence. Maybe she was afraid Tobie might persuade him to marry her without his mother's knowledge. She guessed she could influence him if she really wanted to. Mark was basically weak, and responded to the strongest stimulus. Given time, Tobie was pretty sure she could erase any hesitation from his mind.

But she didn't want that time, and she didn't want Mark. His mother could keep him. However, she couldn't help speculating that there might be another reason for his desertion from duty. Did he think that by staying here, by showing concern for Cilla's father, he might persuade Robert finally to finance his clinic? The precipitation of Mr Jennings' illness might have accelerated his ambitions. Was it unreasonable to suspect that Cilla's father's stroke had made him realise that if Robert did marry Cilla, his expectations need necessarily be greatly reduced?

'Anyway,' Mark was saying now, obviously glad to have got the unpleasant chore of telling her over, 'I've arranged for George to take you back with him in the morning. There's no point in Jim Matheson making the trip, when George is here. He'll be leaving about nine, so he'll take you direct to Hewanorra. . .'

Tobie went to bed soon after that. She needed to get away from all of them, and even the rumbling aftermath of the storm was preferable to Mrs Newman's pretence of bonhomie. In less than twenty-four hours she would be on the plane for London, and she clung to this thought and no other. Away from Emerald Cay, she would be able to think objectively again, and she refused to contemplate the images of what might have been.

The international airport on St Lucia was a busy place. They had landed at Hewanorra two weeks ago, when they arrived in the islands, before driving the several miles to Castries on the northwestern coast. But to reach Emerald Cay they had flown from the smaller, commercial airport at Vigie, which was nearer the capital, and where Jim Matheson would have taken her had she flown with him instead of George Capra.

The American had been very kind, however, escorting her personally to the terminal buildings, and assuring himself that she had no problems before leaving her. If he thought it was strange that Mark had not accompanied her to the airport himself, he made no mention of it, and in all honesty Tobie was glad Mark hadn't. They had nothing further to say to one another, and small talk was beyond her right now.

With her luggage checked in, she still had some time to wait before her flight was due to be called, so she made her way to the airport bookstall. She spent a good half hour studying the latest paperbacks and then, having purchased a rather luridly-jacketed thriller, she bought herself a cup of coffee and sat down to wait.

But she couldn't concentrate. She told herself it was the constant surge of humanity that swelled about her, but in her heart of hearts she knew it was not that at all. She was leaving the islands, that was her real affliction, the malady that made nonsense out of the words on the paper, and drew her eyes irresistibly towards the exits. She was leaving knowing that by doing so she would never see Robert again, and there was a physical ache inside her at the knowledge.

Putting the book away, she finished her coffee and rose to her feet. Perhaps if she cleared passport control, she would feel less restless. Once she had passed through the barrier she would to all intents and purposes have left the island, thus preventing any reckless impulse to remain.

She was making her way towards the controlled area when an angry cry hailed her. She thought at first she must be mistaken, that her inner turmoil had invented an halucinatory voice to torment her. But the hand that reached for her arm and grasped it in a pitiless grip was not an hallucination, and the pain on Robert's face as he struggled to maintain his balance was not an hallucination either. He had evidently been hurrying, judging by the tenor of his breathing, and the effort had almost been too much for him.

'Damn you, Tobie!' he muttered, as she automatically put a supporting arm about him. 'Won't you allow me to keep what little self-respect I have left?'

Tobie drew back again, hurt by the bitterness in his tone, but his hold upon her prevented her from walking away from him. In fact, in the press of people their little altercation went unobserved, and only she was conscious of the angry accusation of his gaze.

'What the hell are you doing?' he demanded, his lean face taut with feeling. 'I asked you not to leave. Is it too much to ask that you might give me a chance to justify myself?'

Tobie stared at him. 'I don't know what you're talking about,' she said at last, stiffly. 'You knew we—*I*—was leaving today. You even said goodbye.'

'I asked you to stay,' he corrected grimly. 'You haven't forgotten what I told you yesterday. I said we would talk, and that is my intention, although God knows I didn't want it to be like this!'

Tobie shook her head. 'You stayed in Castries last night. You told Mark to say goodbye to me—'

'I did *what*!' Robert's expression was eloquent of his disbelief. 'Mark knows exactly what I told him, and wishing you goodbye had no part in it!'

'But—' Tobie moved her shoulders helplessly, 'why would he lie?'

'I can think of half a dozen reasons offhand,' retorted Robert harshly, recovered now and getting restless. 'Come on, we can't talk here. I've got a taxi waiting outside. We'll go back to Castries.'

'But I can't—I mean—my luggage—' Tobie began to protest, and then broke off at the darkening impatience in his eyes. 'Robert, my flight leaves in under an hour. I can't leave the airport. I've already checked in.'

Robert frowned. 'So your cases are on board. That's okay. They can send them back from London. Give me a minute to speak to the stewardess at the desk, then you'll be free to go.'

Tobie licked her lips. 'But there's not another flight until tomorrow!' she exclaimed.

'You won't be taking that either,' retorted Robert shortly, and leaving her, he limped rather more slowly than usual across to the check-in counter.

Tobie did a nervous pirouette as she waited,

her thoughts in a turmoil, her stomach fluttering rather nauseously. She didn't really understand any of this even now, but after the devastation of these last hours, seeing him again was enough—for the moment.

Robert came back to her, lean and familiar in the denim outfit. He had not had an opportunity to change his clothes since yesterday morning, and as her eyes searched his face more closely she doubted he had even been to bed. He looked tired and hollow-cheeked, and lines of exhaustion were etched beside his mouth.

'Okay, that's settled,' he stated, taking her arm forcefully. 'We'll pick your luggage up tomorrow. But right now we have more important things to do.'

'We have?'

Tobie glanced at him anxiously as he urged her towards the glass doors, but he did not respond to her. He was only intent on steering her out to where the cab he had mentioned was waiting, propelling her into the back when the driver opened the door and half falling in beside her.

'You know where we're going, Juan,' he said to the olive-skinned individual behind the wheel, who was grinning at Tobie through the rear-view mirror. 'Remind me I owe you—we made it just in time. Now let's put on some speed.'

'Yes, sir, Mr Lang.' Juan glanced over his shoulder and raised a stubby thumb. 'You just leave it to me. The Hotel Regency, wasn't it? No sooner said than done!'

Even Robert's lips twitched a little at that, but

it was a grim inflection. He looked bone-weary, and Tobie forgot everything else in her concern for him.

'You'll kill yourself if you go on like this,' she protested, once Juan's attention was taken up with his driving. 'I know you're not an invalid, so don't look at me like that, but I'm sure you're not supposed to put so much strain—'

'What would you have had me do?' he demanded, hauling himself up from the slumped position he had assumed after collapsing beside her. 'Do you realise I've spent the last three hours looking for you?'

'Three hours!' Tobie stared at him. 'But—how—you were at the hospital—'

'Correction, I spent the night at the hospital,' he returned harshly. 'I flew back to Emerald Cay this morning. On the plane that was supposed to be taking Mark to Vigie.'

Tobie blinked. 'But I went on the helicopter—'

'I know that now.'

'Didn't Mark tell you?'

'When? This morning—or yesterday afternoon?'

Tobie tried to think. 'Well—yesterday afternoon, I suppose.'

'You forget—so far as I was concerned, you were not leaving.'

Tobie sighed. 'But you must have known—'

'I didn't know anything,' he retorted. 'After the conversation I'd had with Mark, the last thing I expected was that you should walk out on me once again.'

'I wasn't walking out on you!'

'What would you call it, then?' he demanded.

'You were with Cilla. I thought—oh, I thought—'

'I told you on the yacht, Cilla and I mean nothing to one another.'

'She—she may mean nothing to you, but you—'

'Tobie, Cilla's going to marry Jim Matheson. She and I are only friends. Whatever impression you gained, it was the incorrect one.'

'But—' Tobie caught her breath. 'That night— that night the Jennings came to dinner—'

'Yes?'

'You said she had plans to marry you.'

'No, you assumed that,' Robert corrected her harshly. He sighed heavily. 'I'm not denying I let you go on thinking it. After what you said, I wanted to punish you.'

'As you did later?' she reminded him tremulously, and his eyes darkened with sudden emotion.

'Not here, Tobie,' he muttered, with an eloquent glance at the back of Juan's head. 'Don't push me too far. Right now, I'd like to get my hands on you, but I'm afraid I might strangle you for the torture you've put me through, and I don't want any witnesses!'

Tobie trembled. 'At—at least tell me what you want of me,' she begged, half afraid of the passion in his face, and with a groan of self-disgust he pulled her into his arms.

'What do you think I want of you?' he

demanded hoarsely, against her ear. 'God, Tobie, I love you. I want to live with you for the rest of my life—if you can stand it.'

CHAPTER ELEVEN

IF I can——' she started, only to be silenced by the hungry pressure of his mouth. Ignoring Juan, and the delighted glances he was making in his mirror, Robert kissed her with all the eager urgency of his nature, crushing her back against the leather upholstery, his hand possessively gripping her waist. He kissed her long and searchingly, making her insistently aware of what he was feeling.

'Satisfied?' he muttered at last, lifting his mouth only inches from hers, and Tobie slipped her arms around his neck.

'Not nearly,' she mouthed, for his eyes alone, and with a determined effort, he dragged himself back from her, his breathing laboured.

'Later,' he grated, staring grimly through the car's windows. Then: 'Is this the best you can do, Morales?'

'There's a speed limit, Mr Lang, sir,' Juan protested, though his eyes still danced. 'But I'll do what I can.'

Impatient for the journey to be over, Tobie was a mass of nerves by the time they reached the imposing entrance to the Hotel Regency. When the major-domo opened the taxi door for her she got out rather jerkily, then hung about indecisively as Robert struggled to emerge. She would have liked to help him, only the hard line of his mouth at the evident effort it was taking deterred her, and it was left to the commissionaire to summon assistance.

To Robert's obvious indignity, a wheelchair was provided, and he was helped into it. Only then did he look up and meet Tobie's eyes, and the expression on his face left her weak with compassion. It was compounded of pain and weariness and complete frustration, and she knew there was nothing she could say to assuage his feelings.

The reception clerk evidently knew him, and the formalities were brief. Tobie didn't know what arrangements Robert had made, or indeed in what capacity she was registered. She only knew that a porter was summoned to escort them to their rooms, and they crossed the marble foyer to the lifts.

Their rooms were on the tenth floor. When the porter inserted the key and swung open the double doors, Tobie saw that they had been given a suite, and the elegant luxury of it all almost took her breath away. Preceding Robert into the cream and green opulence of a drawing room, she saw that from the long windows they had a magnificent view of the ocean, with the town and harbour away to the right. There was a beach below the hotel, and at this hour of the afternoon there were still sunbathers in the shade of the conically thatched roofs of the beach huts, lazily soaking up the last of the day. It was a perfect place for lovers, and as the door closed behind the porter she turned eagerly back to Robert.

'It's—beautiful,' she exclaimed helplessly. 'I can hardly believe I'm here!'

Robert's expression was not encouraging as he manoeuvred the wheelchair across the shell-coloured carpeting. 'It's adequate,' he conceded, cursing when a rug impeded his progress. 'The manager is a friend of mine.'

'Oh, I see.' His attitude affected Tobie's enthusiasm. 'Anyway,' she added, half defensively, 'I like it. But then, as you would doubtless agree, I'm not much used to such things.'

Robert gave her a hard look, then swung his chair about and headed for a door across the room. 'This is one of the bedrooms,' he said, without answering her. 'There's a bathroom beyond, and if you don't mind, I think I'll take a bath. I only had time to wash and shave at Soledad. I didn't even change my clothes.'

Tobie nodded. 'All right. Is there anything I can do? Do you want me to help you?'

'No!' he snapped savagely. 'You—relax! Read a magazine. You'll find some in that cabinet over there.'

Tobie watched him negotiate the narrow doorway into the bedroom, and then paced restlessly across the room. Its delicate beauty had lost its charm, however, and the whole day seemed to have gone sour on her. Why? What had she done? They had seemed close for those few minutes in the taxi. Had she imagined Robert's impassioned declaration of his love for her?

Standing by the window, she tried to make sense of it all, and when understanding came to

her, she was amazed at her own lack of percep-
tion. Was she so blind to his feelings after all
this time? Hadn't she watched his humiliation for
herself? It was this that had left him feeling raw
and indignant, impatient with his weakness, and
impatient with her for witnessing it.

Leaving the window, she kicked off her sandals
and walked silently through into the bedroom. It
was another spacious apartment, with yellow silk
curtains at the windows and a soft lemon carpet
underfoot. All the units and the bedhead were
white, and padded with satin, while the coverlet
on the bed was figured white damask.

To her surprise, a dark suit was laid on the
bed, along with a pristine white shirt, and ignoring
for a moment the sounds coming from the adjoining bathroom, Tobie opened a door of the tall
closet. As she half expected, other men's clothes
were hanging there, and she realised Robert must
keep this suite for when he was in Castries. It
made it a more personal place somehow, not just
a hotel bedroom, and her tongue appeared to
moisten her lips as she stepped towards the
bathroom door.

It was not locked, and she turned the handle
quietly, not wishing to startle him. Like the bedroom and the drawing room, the bathroom was
huge, and the bath itself, a circular basin in the
middle of the floor, was filled with soapy water.
The wheelchair had been pushed carelessly
towards a shower cubicle, and Robert was sitting
in the bath, with his back towards the door. He
was in the process of soaping his arms, and

although there were mirrors, they were steamy. and he didn't observe her barefoot approach.

Tobie knelt down on the tiles beside the bath. It was a tantalising experience, having him at her mercy like this, and she was half reluctant to expose herself. She enjoyed watching him, though she acknowledged he might not approve of her so doing.

Unable to resist any longer, she stroked her fingernail across his shoulder, and his involuntary move exposed the scars along his spine she had made the day before. He swung round in the spacious basin, confronting her with angry eyes, but she was too much in love with him to be deterred by anything he might say.

'This is nice,' she said huskily, her gesture describing their surroundings. 'I gather you've stayed here before. You didn't tell me that.'

'It's useful to have somewhere private,' he conceded tautly, shifting in the water. 'And I thought you'd prefer this to going back to Soledad right away. But if you'd rather—'

'Oh, no. No!' Tobie shook her head. 'Not Soledad,' she demurred unsteadily, and his eyes darkened at the implied protest.

'I shan't be long,' he muttered now. 'Then we can talk. There's a lot to be said, a lot to be explained.'

Tobie hesitated. 'Do you want me to go? Or do you want me to help you? I could wash your back—in mitigation for those scratches I inflicted, if you like. I'm quite good in the bathroom. At least, that's what Laura's twins tell me.'

'You're quite good at bathing children, is that what you mean?' enquired Robert tightly, and she sighed.

'No. Laura's twins are seven. They're quite capable of bathing themselves. We—we have fun together, that's all.' She paused. 'Why don't you want me to help you, Robert? I love you. Don't push me away.'

His long lashes lowered, hiding the expression in his eyes. 'Even like this?' he demanded violently. 'Knowing what a physical wreck I am? Oh, Tobie, if only I hadn't been such a bloody fool!'

'I—I'd second that,' she murmured unsteadily, stretching out her hand towards him. 'So don't—don't be a bloody fool now! Don't you know it's you I care about—the man you are? Not the shell that gives you existence!'

He moved then, kneeling in front of her, burying his face in the hands she so tentatively offered. 'I can't let you go, I can't!' he muttered in an anguished voice, and her heart lurched inside her. 'Without you, it's only half a life, and I can't take it any longer.'

'I don't want you to take it,' she whispered huskily. 'I want you to take *me*! As God's my witness, no one else ever has.'

With a sound of impatience he got to his feet, and although she protested, he stepped out on to the rim of the basin, swaying slightly as he did so. 'I'm not paralysed,' he stated, reaching for a towel and wrapping it about himself. 'Give me that bathrobe, will you? Then maybe we can say what has to be said before we go too far.'

Tobie got obediently to her feet, handing him the fleecy robe that was hanging behind the door. Its dark brown colouring accentuated his darkness, as well as the pallor of his face, and she had to steel herself not to follow its contours with her hands and use herself as a shield to protect him. She ached to touch him, to feel his arms about her and his mouth on hers. But Robert's determination deterred her, and she went back into the bedroom at his command.

He followed her slowly, reaching the bed with evident difficulty, and on impulse she stopped him there. 'Why can't we stay here?' she suggested, indicating its generous proportions. 'You can relax, and we can talk.' She gazed at him appealingly. 'Mmm?'

Robert lounged on to the end of the bed, looking at her through narrowed eyes. 'All right,' he said, with a sigh, acknowledging his own weakness. 'I'll admit, I am tired. But that's mostly because I didn't get any sleep last night.'

'You didn't?' Tobie's lips parted in sympathy, then she made an anxious sound. 'I didn't ask you—how is Mr Jennings? I'm afraid I forgot all about him.'

Robert shook his head. 'He's a sick man, but he's known that for some time.'

Tobie frowned. 'I thought he had a stroke.'

'He did. But that's not what I meant.' Robert bent his head. 'Harvey has cancer. He's had it for the past five years. He knows he's dying, and now he doesn't care when.'

'Now?'

'Now that Cilla and Jim have finally got together,' explained Robert quietly. 'That trip to Miami—you remember?' She nodded. 'I did have a meeting with Rowan Hartley, but primarily it was an opportunity for Jim and Cilla to see something of one another, away from the island.' His lips twisted. 'I guess you saw it differently.'

'You know I did,' exclaimed Tobie hotly, sitting down beside him, her eyes wide and indignant. 'And you knew I would, didn't you?' she insisted, brushing his robe aside and gripping his knee with her hand. 'You wanted to make me jealous!'

'Did I succeed?' he asked humorously, letting her have her way. But as her fingers crept higher, he stilled their intimate progress. 'Tobie, we have to talk, and when you do that—'

'Does it bother you?' she breathed, but he put her firmly away from him and moved back on the bed.

'Anyway,' he continued, ignoring the disappointed signals her eyes were making, 'Harvey recovered consciousness, but he's very weak. The doctors are not optimistic, and that was why I stayed with Cilla last night. Jim was away, he had a charter to the States, but he's back now, so I was able to leave them.'

'I see.' Tobie sobered. 'I'm sorry. Mark led me to believe—'

'We'll get to Mark in a minute,' said Robert heavily. 'First there's something I must tell you. It was without doubt my mother who sent you away from the hospital.'

Tobie gazed at him. 'Was it?'

'Yes.' He shook his head. 'Will you forgive me?'

'Of course.' Tobie wriggled back beside him, the hem of her dress working up above her knees. 'How did you find out? Not Mark!' She blinked. 'I thought he didn't know.'

'He doesn't. Or at least, I'm pretty sure not,' declared Robert flatly. Then he frowned. 'Will you pass me the pants I dropped over there?'

'The jeans?' Tobie grimaced. 'Of course.' She scrambled off the bed, picked up the jeans, and climbed on again. 'Here you are.'

'Thanks.' Robert gave her a half smile, rummaging in the back pocket and bringing out a folded sheet of paper. 'Take a look at that,' he advised her, dropping the jeans again. 'Tell me what you think.'

Tobie opened the sheet of paper slowly, and as she did so her own image appeared before her, a delicate charcoal drawing, that captured the warm beauty of her classically-boned features.

She gazed at it wide-eyed for several seconds, then she looked up at him speechlessly. It was the most precious thing she had ever been given, the gift of Robert's love.

'I did it last night,' he told her gently. 'Sitting at Harvey's bedside. Cilla said she liked it.'

Tobie shook her head, pressing her lips together to stop their trembling. 'It—it's very flattering,' she said, looking at it again, but Robert shook his head.

'It's you,' he said firmly, taking it from her

and studying it himself. 'And it should prove once
and for all that you're never out of my mind.'

Tobie's heart was in her eyes. 'Oh, Robert!'
she breathed, and he folded the paper again with
hands that trembled.

'I have to tell you,' he said, but it was obviously an effort for him not to touch her, 'this little
picture is proof to me that my mother is at the
bottom of all this.'

Tobie shook her head bewilderedly. 'It is?'

'Yes.' He expelled his breath slowly. 'Yesterday afternoon, during the conversation I had with
Mark, he admitted that Mother had told him she'd
seen you before—in a painting in my studio.'

'Yes?' Tobie still didn't see the connection.

'Well, she couldn't have,' he said flatly. 'Until
I drew this little sketch last night I didn't have a
picture of you.'

Tobie stared at him. 'But you must have done!
I mean—you sketched me—'

'—dozens of times,' he conceded gently. 'And
I painted you, at least twice.' He paused. 'But I
destroyed them all.'

'You destroyed them?' Tobie swallowed convulsively, and now he reached for her hand.

'Yes,' he said quietly, 'I burned them all. As
soon as I could get my hands on them.'

'Robert!'

'Imagine, if you can, how I felt,' he begged
her softly. 'So far as I knew, you hadn't even
bothered to come and see me! I was in a pretty
low state, partially paralysed, or so I believed,
and the only person I truly cared about had run

out on me. Oh, yes——' this as she endeavoured to pull away from him, 'that was what I thought. And when I found out about the baby. . .'

Tobie stared at him. 'When did you find out about the baby?'

Robert held her gaze with his. 'Oh, I suppose it must have been about two weeks after the accident.'

'Two weeks!' Tobie made a helpless gesture. 'But you said——your mother——'

'My mother didn't tell me, someone else did. A private investigator I had hired to find you. Only he didn't——find you, I mean. After——after losing the baby, you apparently went away, and short of approaching your sister, he had no way of finding out where.'

'Oh, Robert!' Tobie slumped. 'What must you have thought?'

'You know what I thought,' he said simply. 'Your apparent disregard for what had happened to me——losing the baby; I thought you'd decided to get out of London so I shouldn't find you.'

Tobie shook her head. 'It wasn't like that.'

'I know it now.' Robert caressed her fingers. 'I realise losing the baby must have been a blow. You were right to go away. A change of scene was what you needed.'

Tobie shook her head. 'You don't understand,' she said, biting so hard on her lower lip she almost drew blood. 'I didn't go away——at least, not in the way you imagine.' She hesitated. 'Have you ever heard of a place called Riderbeck?'

Robert frowned. 'I can't say that I have.

Why? What is it? A hostel of some sort?'

Tobie almost smiled. 'It's a mental institution,' she got out chokingly. 'A psychiatric hospital. I spent six months there.'

Robert drew back to look into her strained face. 'My God! Why?'

Tobie sniffed. 'I—I had a nervous breakdown. I couldn't eat, I couldn't sleep, I didn't talk: it was a complete collapse.' She quivered beneath his gaze. 'Does it make a difference?'

'Of course it makes a difference!' he muttered, in a strangled voice. 'Oh, Tobie, Tobie! If only I'd known!' He gave up his attempt at detachment and hauled her into his arms. 'My darling, I'd give anything to be able to go back and start again, but as I can't, I can only promise you it will never happen again.'

Tobie's tears mingled with drops of water that ran down her cheek from his damp hair, but she was unaware of them. Robert was holding her, kissing her, telling her in a thousand different ways that he loved her, and all the anxiety of the past melted beneath his ardent caress.

'God, I could kill my mother for that,' he muttered, his face buried in the hollow between her breasts. 'But at least I think I know why she did it, although God knows it's no excuse.'

Tobie parted the lapels of his bathrobe so that the hair on his chest brushed her breasts. 'So long as we're together now, that's all that matters,' she breathed, as his fingers loosened the last buttons of her bodice. 'Mmm, darling, you smell delicious.'

Robert's breathing had quickened, but he pulled himself up from her, cupping her breast in his cool brown fingers. 'If only you'd told me about the baby that day at the apartment,' he exclaimed, 'instead of pretending you were planning to leave me.'

Tobie gasped. 'I didn't do that!'

'Not in so many words, perhaps, but I thought I knew the implication. You said you wanted us to make a commitment, that you wanted marriage or nothing. And I, poor fool that I was, had only seen marriage as the hell my father's had been.'

Tobie raised her hands to his cheeks. 'Oh, Robert, if only you'd told me that! If only you hadn't got so angry!'

He shook his head. 'I guess it was resentment, more than anger,' he admitted. 'I didn't care for the hold you were getting on me. I wasn't used to it, and I rebelled.'

Tobie hesitated. 'Why did you talk to Mark yesterday?'

'Oh—' Reluctantly, Robert released her and rolled on to his back, staring up at the ceiling. 'Well, I wanted to tell him that you wouldn't be leaving with him. I was going to admit that we already knew one another, and that, if you'd have me, I was going to ask you to marry me.'

'But you said—'

'I know what I said. But during the course of that Godawful day I realised I had to have you, whatever you'd done.'

'Mark and I were never lovers,' Tobie assured him.

'I know that. I knew it at the time I made love to you on the yacht. I knew no other man had touched you. I just wanted to hurt you, as you'd intended to hurt me.'

'By coming here? But you invited me.'

'Yes, I did. Mother wasn't keen, as you can imagine. But as soon as I found out who you were, I knew I had to see you. I'd have moved heaven and earth to achieve that.'

'And when you did see me?'

He turned his head to smile at her. 'I fell in love with you all over again.'

Tobie rolled on to her stomach beside him, running her hand lightly across his flat stomach. 'Poor Mark!'

'Poor Mark, nothing. He and his mother have done their best to ruin my life.'

Tobie bent her head. 'Did you tell him— everything?'

'As much as was necessary to prove I meant what I said.' Robert hesitated. 'I think I've limited his expectations, if that's the right word. You realise, don't you, that all Mark really wants is money?'

Tobie nodded. 'He wants to specialise.'

'So he said. Unfortunately, I don't think he has the ability.'

'I still don't understand why your mother hated me so much.'

'Don't you?' Robert's eyes grew lazy. 'She probably saw you as a threat. I was very ill, remember. I might have died. Imagine how frustrating it would have been if I'd insisted on a deathbed marriage ceremony!'

'Robert!'

'Well!' he was unrepentant. 'I'm right, aren't I?' And remembering that Mrs Newman had suspected she was pregnant, it was not so unreasonable. One day she would tell Robert about that. But not now. Not today.

'But why did Mark let me go? When he knew what you'd said?'

'Ah, yes, the final insult,' murmured Robert, with a sigh. 'It probably has to do with the fact that I didn't respond to his little attempt at extortion.'

'Extortion!' Tobie was appalled. 'You mean— money? How could he do that?'

'He couldn't.' Robert grimaced. 'But he tried. Unfortunately, I wasn't interested in his threats to make my condition public. You see, I knew what their idea was all along. It pains me to say it, but they might well have been right. It was a reasonable assumption that I might not recover. Until I found out that Mark was dating you, I'd been pretty apathetic, but after that I determined to get well.' He made a rueful gesture. 'But as you see, I haven't succeeded.'

'You're well enough for me,' Tobie whispered, bending to caress his chest with her lips. 'What are you going to do about them now?'

Robert lifted her chin, his expression eloquent of what her teasing lips were doing to him. 'I don't know,' he said huskily. 'What can I do?'

'Mark hasn't gone back to London, as you probably know,' Tobie ventured gently. 'Perhaps he ought to stay with his mother, as they depend upon one another so much.'

Robert grimaced. 'Should I let him build his clinic?' he speculated softly. 'It's one way of ensuring that my mother leaves Emerald Cay. I pity his poor patients, that's all.'

'He had no time for Mr Jennings,' mused Tobie thoughtfully, and Robert nodded.

'I know. Of course, he never examined him, so he didn't know about the cancer. All he saw the Jennings as was a drain on my resources.' Robert let Tobie untie the cord on his robe. 'If he'd only known, they were my lifeline, the only real friends I had.'

Tobie moved over him. 'I'm your friend,' she breathed, tasting his lips. 'Is that the talking over?'

Robert half smiled. 'One last thing. Why did you come to Emerald Cay? Was it for revenge?'

Tobie hesitated. 'I can't deny a certain desire to see you squirm when you saw me and Mark together,' she admitted honestly. 'Only it didn't work out like that, did it?'

'How did it work out?' he probed, easing her dress off her shoulders. 'Hell, I'm going to tear this, but it doesn't matter. I'll buy you a dozen new ones.'

'You're a brute,' she teased huskily, as the material shredded. Then: 'You know how it worked out. I was as jealous as any other woman scorned by the man she loved.'

'Scorned?' With her slender body exposed to his satisfaction, he uttered a low rueful laugh.

'Oh, Tobie, if you'd only known! You don't know what it was like pretending to be indifferent. And that night I came to your bedroom *I* suffered agonies by denying you.'

'Did you?' Her lips opened over his, and with exclamation he rolled over, imprisoning her beneath him. 'Oh, Robert, I thought you were tired!'

'I can sleep later,' he told her thickly, finding the swollen fullness of her breast. 'Right now, we've got a lot of time to make up.'

And she could only agree.

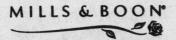

MILLS & BOON®

Anne Mather

COLLECTOR'S EDITION

If you have missed any of the previously published titles in the Anne Mather Collector's Edition, you may order them by sending a cheque or postal order (please do not send cash) made payable to Harlequin Mills & Boon Ltd. for £2.99 per book plus 50p per book postage and packing. Please send your order to: Anne Mather Collector's Edition, P.O. Box 236, Croydon, Surrey, CR9 3RU (EIRE: Anne Mather Collector's Edition, P.O. Box 4546, Dublin 24).

1 JAKE HOWARD'S WIFE
2 SCORPIONS' DANCE
3 CHARADE IN WINTER
4 A FEVER IN THE BLOOD
5 WILD ENCHANTRESS
6 SPIRIT OF ATLANTIS
7 LOREN'S BABY
8 DEVIL IN VELVET
9 LIVING WITH ADAM
10 SANDSTORM